The Great Chicago Fire Conspiracy

AIRSHIP 27 PRODUCTIONS

The Great Chicago Fire Conspiracy
© 2021 George Tackes

Published by Airship 27 Productions

www.airship27.com
www.airship27hangar.com

Cover illustration © 2021 Chris Rawding
Interior illustrations © 2021 Gary Kato

Editor: Ron Fortier
Associate Editor: Jonathan Sweet
Production designer: Rob Davis
Marketing and Promotions Manager: Michael Vance

ISBN: 978-1-953589-11-8

Produced in the United States of America

10 9 8 7 6 5 4 3 2 1

THE GREAT CHICAGO FIRE CONSPIRACY

CONSPIRACY

BY GEORGE TACKES

Dedicated to Kay, Kerry, and Jill

ACKNOWLEDGEMENTS:

Although this is a work of fiction, it weaves in many reported incidents from newspapers accounts and the official inquiry. In this regard, my gratitude extends to:

The Essential Great Chicago Fire by William Pack—The spark that ignited *The Great Chicago Fire Conspiracy*.

Also the heavy winds and dry autumn provided by:

The Great Chicago Fire by Robert Cromie (thrilling and fundamental)

The Great Chicago Fire and The Myth of Mrs. O'Leary's Cow by Richard F. Bales (a scholarly account but nonetheless entertaining)

CHAPTER 1

"The Civil War is over."

Speaking that simple truth resulted in a punch to the face. More specifically, a fist to the left temple but it didn't matter. The consequence was the same. More punches and kicks followed, and the dark-haired former soldier was rendered unconscious by two unwashed men. After a final kick to the stomach, they left.

Reminding Confederate sympathizers that the Civil War was over opened old wounds that the Confederacy lost. And that typically provoked a violent reaction. This time it was meant to.

For almost a quarter of an hour, former United States Army Second Lieutenant Philip Avers lie sprawled amidst the heart of Chicago's underworld, Conley's Patch.

A vice-ridden slum, Conley's Patch, radiated over several blocks. Its wickedness and immorality oozed out from its center. Its center was the block that bordered on Monroe and Adams on the north and south and Market and Fifth Streets—although locals still called it Wells Street—on the west and east. Dirty, ramshackle shanty after dirty, ramshackle shanty tightly packed the landscape. Broken wooden pallets functioned as cheap fencing. A squalid hub for social outcasts and criminals of all sorts inhabited this section a couple blocks east of the south branch of the Chicago River.

No one noticed or acknowledged the disheveled, dark-haired man in rumpled brown clothes crumpled outside the back room of the abandoned hovel near the corner of Monroe and Adams Streets. They merely stepped over or around him like any other piece of garbage in the street.

In the muck, various smells roused Avers from his stupor. The foul, acrid stench like the bottom of a garbage can filled his thin nostrils and forced his eyes open.

Avers sat up slowly recovering from the beating. The beating confirmed what he suspected. The men still believed the Confederate States would rise again and the man he was searching for was still in Chicago.

For nearly six and a half years, Avers had been tracking a murderer—a fugitive that every public official, federal and state, declared was dead.

He was part of the military detachment which surrounded and tried to capture him alive. They set the barn on fire but the man refused to come out. The popular story was that an NCO disobeyed orders and shot the killer. The Army sergeant shot and killed someone. But Avers was never convinced that the body recovered was the actual murderer. Flames disfigured the body just enough.

The official statement from Washington was the man was killed by the U.S. Army. The newly assigned lieutenant disagreed. Ultimately, he had to resign his commission to track that man down and bring him to justice.

He chased the killer from the East coast to the South to the Hawaiian Islands. Then the trail led from a sanctuary there to Europe, specifically Germany and England.

During his dogged pursuit there, he stumbled upon and thwarted a plot by radicals to drag America into the Franco-Prussian War.

While in Europe, Avers happened upon the murdered man's family. In England, the murdered man's wife and son encountered the murderer. Avers came to their rescue before the murderer could inflict any harm to them. Although cornered, the killer narrowly escaped Avers.

The killer's trail led back to America. The three of them had lost the trail once back on their native soil. No trace of the killer existed despite Avers' trained eye and years of experience chasing this man. It was as if death had finally apprehended him instead of Avers.

That July, the killer made a mistake and revealed his location. He murdered the son of the man he assassinated because the boy and his mother once again encountered him but this time in Chicago. They recognized him and despite his protestations they knew it was him. His face haunted them. His face was etched in the wife's mind for more than six years, etched in their minds. The son only physically encountered the killer months before in Europe so the killer's face was still fresh in his mind.

Their first response was to alert Avers who traveled to the dry Midwestern city from Washington, D.C. He was briefing former military colleagues in the nation's capital about its near involvement in the Franco-Prussian War. He left D.C. as soon as he received word. By the time he arrived in Chicago, the boy was dead. The boy's mother and Avers knew he was murdered and the identity of the murderer. Avers was determined to have the final showdown!

The murderer made his fateful mistake.

It was an unusually warm October in the Midwest. Not so typical of this time of year. It was warm and dry. It hadn't rained for weeks, less than ten inches since the boy's death. All of which increased the stench in Conley's Patch to act on Avers like smelling salts.

Avers had sufficiently recovered from the beating to follow his assailants, members of the Ku Klux Klan. And the Ku Klux Klan had known ties to the murderer.

Bloodied and bruised, Avers strained to pick himself off the wooden footpath. The smell of urine and rat feces lingered in his nostrils. His attackers left but he knew where to find them. He had been shadowing them for a few days. He confirmed where their sympathies lay with his beating.

The War-Between-The-States ended less than ten years ago so it was still fresh in Americans' minds and hearts. It wasn't difficult to start a discussion or argument about it. Everyone still maintained a strong opinion and no compunction to share it.

Some Confederate sympathizers could get very violent about it. Usually ones with staunch connections to Confederate soldiers craved revenge – demanding retribution for Northern reprisal. These men were definitely members of such a faction.

Two men had beaten him up. He didn't resist. The thrashing needed to end soon so he could follow them. The quickest way, he knew from experience, to end a fight was to lose.

He leaned against the hovel's wooden wall to hoist his sore, aching body. The pain was worth it. He'd recover quickly enough. These men would lead him to the fugitive murderer. One of them was probably providing him shelter in Conley's Patch.

Wherever the fugitive was hidden, Avers would learn of it tonight. He was sure of it. Informants suggested a gathering of Ku Klux Klan members in Chicago. The Klan had been under surveillance by the federal government for months. They were angry and planning something. Ever since President Grant signed the Ku Klux Klan Act in April, retaliation was in the works. But sources had been wrong before, and even purposely deceptive.

Avers picked up his derby knocked into the corner when the first punch was thrown. It was brown and dirty and scuffed like the rest of his clothes. He needed to blend in. He needed to look like every other denizen of Conley's Patch.

He gently placed the derby atop his greasy black hair and ran his hand down his moustache to his scruffy chin. He hadn't shaved for a couple days.

The men headed west. He watched them through blurry eyes after the final kick was thrust into his stomach.

Avers pulled the derby down hard on his head and made a beeline south on Market Street. He disregarded any hoots or come ons from the occasional hooker. He knew where the men went. They visited the same place for the last two nights. A wooden planked sidewalk led the way to a saloon near Quincy Street. The oaken sign nailed to the front door read, "Sunset Inn."

CHAPTER 2

His contacts within military intelligence described Sunset Inn as a popular hangout for mild dissidents, individuals very annoyed at government interference of their chosen professions. Their chosen professions profited from theft, murder, extortion, kidnapping, prostitution, and that ilk.

Removing his dusty sport coat, tossing it aside, Avers stepped inside and no one reacted. Not even the bartender, an unwashed, overweight brute in a stained undershirt. He barely reacted even when Avers quietly ordered a beer. He developed a taste for it when he was in Germany. Most of the patrons were drinking whiskey.

He scanned the saloon. An unpolished wooden counter ran along one side with wobbly stools and even more wobbly patrons sitting on them. People filled the rickety tables with mismatched hardwood chairs occupied the other side. A metal pole centered the saloon. The floor was slate and chipped with pock marks like the bartender's face.

Leaning against the bar, he spotted his two attackers at the table furthest from the door. His recent bashing enhanced his camouflage. He staggered to the pole and leaned against it for support with his back to the men. He intended to listen to them talk. But they did not utter a single word.

Both of them had limp brown hair and dark brown moustaches. Their sports jackets and trousers were brown and dirty. Like him, their clothes did very little to distinguish themselves from each other or the other bar patrons.

Facial hair was the only feature to distinguish patrons from one another—chevron moustaches, pencil moustaches, walrus moustaches and imperial moustaches. Paint brushes. Goatees, ducktail short box beards. Some trimmed. Some untrimmed.

Once again he sized up his assailants. One man was tall, muscular, and thick. The other was medium height and build. Bad teeth did not contrast them from anyone else. What did separate them from the other was that they had no scars on their faces or hands.

A lean and athletic-looking man made a grand entrance from the back room and joined them. He looked a little older than the two other men, but not by much.

In all these years, he never changed his appearance. His jet-black hair and chevron moustache were well-groomed. His bearing was aristocratic. Today he wore a sable frock coat, felt derby, beige suit, and paisley ascot.

Avers knew the man's manner had been cultivated from his years on the stage. He knew the man was thirty-three years old. He knew that he lacked any aristocratic breeding and his parents were married thirteen years after he was born.

The badly-etched J.W.B. hand-drawn tattoo on his left hand and a dis-figured right thumb confirmed his identity for Avers. The scar on the back of his neck corroborated it.

Avers discovered John Wilkes Booth did not die at the hands of Sgt. Boston Corbett in that barn in Port Royal, Virginia on April 26, 1865. Despite the official proclamation, Booth did not die twelve days after Abraham Lincoln. The 16th New York Calvary Regiment actually failed in its mission

Once again he was mere feet from his quarry. He shuddered at the arrogance of the man.

Lincoln's assassin calmly ordered a drink as he flirted with the buck-toothed barmaid with a pleasant face. She enjoyed it with a smile at the handsome man. She like almost everyone else in the saloon was oblivious of the notorious villain in their midst.

Six years taught Avers patience. He wanted to kill Booth right there. How he wished he was still in possession of his Army saber. The knife he had hidden in his wrist sheath could be used to quickly dispose of the fiend. He didn't care whether his companions or other patrons retaliated. He shifted the knife to his belt sheath.

He preferred if Booth was arrested for the murder of Tad and hung for his crimes.

CHAPTER 3

Wwhat Avers wanted was the proof that Booth had murdered Lincoln's son. Mary Todd Lincoln and Thomas "Tad" Lincoln came back from Europe with Avers. Mary and Tad returned to their life in Chicago when Avers reported to Washington. The boy was maturing into a fine, young man, partially from Avers' influence. During Chicago's Independence Day celebration, the Lincolns encountered Booth. Eighteen year old Tad boldly confronted him but the accused man calmly defused the situation and tried to put him off. Tad was persistent. By the time, Mary made her way to her son's side; the man had Tad by the throat. Mary fumed as she looked upon the countenance of John Wilkes Booth once again. He shoved Tad into Mary and disappeared in the crowd. Mary immediately sent word to her dear friend, Philip.

On Saturday morning of July 15, Thomas "Tad" Lincoln, the youngest child of Abraham and Mary, died in the Clifton House in Chicago. Cause of death could never be definitively confirmed. Doctors' opinions ranged from tuberculosis to congestive heart failure.

Avers instinctively knew Booth was responsible. He didn't know how, but he did not doubt it.

After greeting each other, Booth and his comrades started to complain about laws that the federal government enacted against the Ku Klux Klan.

In fact, their Southern drawl was how Avers managed to hone in on their conversation amid the cacophony in the bar. He could manage to stand several feet away and still distinguish their conversation.

"Just last week this Chicago rag publishes lies about Ku-Klux committing 'atrocities'," said the tall man as he took a swig out of his glass mug.

"Allegedly committed, my good sir," Booth emphasized. His Southern drawl was quite pronounced. Being a native New Englander, Booth obviously was trying to make himself relatable to his Confederate associates.

"Shit, the headline screamed, 'The Ku-Klux Convictions,' instead praising our actions like the damn fools they are," said the third man, whose Southern accent was subtle but noticeable.

"Mind your manners, gentlemen. Remember we represent the Confederacy in this fair city," Booth articulated as if he were performing on stage.

"You mean this god-forsaken city."

"Not yet," Booth smirked. "Not quite yet."

"Shit, John," the not-as-tall man started to say when Booth leaned over and grabbed his chin.

"No names, fool! No names."

"Sorry. I just get so riled of shitheads besmirching our patriotism."

"And that drunken fool, Grant, shoves a law down the Klan's throat. It's more than a Confederate gentleman can tolerate. Calling it the Ku Klux Klan Act, adding further insult to injury," Booth grumbled.

"Shit. What is habitual corpse anyway?"

"Habeas corpus, my good sir. It is yet another step to strip Americans, specifically the glorious South, of our sublime lifestyle, our exalted liberty, and our individual rights," Booth explained with a flourish.

"Well, whatever it is. We'll avenge our country against this Northern aggression," the tall man said.

"I have been performing a great deal of reconnaissance for my leading role of the plan. Everything else, everyone is in place for tomorrow?" Booth asked.

"As far as I know."

Booth glared at him.

"I'll get confirmation," the tall man said sheepishly.

"I'll get confirmation. Need I remind you, this is appropriate retribution for Sherman's March to the Sea, the burning of Atlanta. But first, tonight, a little personal matter for preparation of tomorrow's festivities. It's only a little ways from here. Something to stoke the flames as it were." Booth grinned and finished his drink.

Avers' plan to simply capture Booth just became more difficult. He felt duty bound to learn about this revenge plan. He needed to alert his former military colleagues. He strained to listen to any more details.

The three men spoke softly but laughed loudly. That's when their Southern accent became obvious and annoyed the regulars. A Southern accent can make a direct association with the Confederacy and Confederate sympathizers were not welcome in the "Land of Lincoln."

Sensing the animosity in the saloon, the three men left money and exited. Avers followed.

CHAPTER 4

Despite being well after 10 p.m., Chicagoans were out and about on this very dark, hot autumn night. The three men chatted softly as they walked along the raised wooden sidewalks north on Market Street and turned the corner at Adams. The elevated sidewalks protected citizens from mud, dirt, and horse debris while they trudged through the dusty roads. Not many streets in Chicago were cobblestones or brick-laden. The "Southern gentlemen" hiked over the Chicago River's southern branch to Canal Street. They turned south.

Avers maintained a respectable distance so he was unable to hear what they were planning. Crossing the Adams Street Bridge would have been difficult without being noticed if the trio hadn't been so intense in their conversation. If the greasy smell of the river's refuse didn't distract them, not much else would. They passed saloon after saloon amid lumberyards, coal sheds, and other small factories of various sorts.

Avers almost lost them as they crossed the overpass above the Fort Wayne and Pittsburgh Railroad tracks.

The moonlight merged with gas street lights threatening to reveal his presence behind them. He stepped off the wooden sidewalk to stroll in the road. The dirt muffled his steps. He thought they might get suspicious so when they stopped at the corner of Adams and Canal Streets. Keeping his head down, Avers passed them and staggered into a saloon at the northwest corner. After entering, he tossed his derby aside on a nearby table.

"Here, what's the meaning of this," said the drunk sitting there.

Avers ignored him and exited as quickly as he entered.

The conspirators meandered a block and a half south and eventually paused in the middle of the block between Jackson and Van Buren.

In the moonlight, Avers saw Booth disappear behind the two men. Avers heard some glass break. The two men just stood there looking out to the street.

Avers staggered like a drunken man toward the tall man and his medium-sized compatriot. Above their heads, an ornately painted framed hanging sign read, "Lull and Holmes Planing Mill." It was a two-story brick building. As Avers got closer, the tall man recognized him.

"Hey, you're the Yankee we whipped earlier."

"Guess we're gonna have to learn you another lesson 'bout respect, shithead."

The tall man threw the first punch. This time Avers wasn't looking to end the fight quickly. He easily ducked the fist.

A kick to the gut for the tall man and upper cut to the medium-sized man were enough to make the two pause. Avers slid a knife out of his belt sheath. Seeing the two-inch blade made the men snicker. Their hesitation provided enough time for Avers to strike again. Gripping the knife's handle, he filled his fist to strengthen his blows. A right cross knocked back the tall man. His head stuck the corner of the doorway. His body went limp and slid down. Two quick jabs, a right then the left, to the chin took out the other one. Both were most definitely stunned if not knocked senseless.

As he proudly overlooked his handiwork, Avers slid the knife back into its sheath. He was struck by a blow from behind but did not lose consciousness. He was shoved face first into the grungy street. Stirring up the dust in the road, fine dirt got in his eyes and mouth.

Gasping for air for a minute, he spit out dirt. After he wiped more grime out of his eyes, he looked around and saw nothing but the two-by-four used to hit him. Looking left and right, he could see nothing but saloons, lumber yards, other small businesses and a few dwellings. No sign of anyone around including Booth or his cohorts.

All was quiet and peaceful along the street. As if nothing dangerous was lurking inside the building in front of him.

Avers glanced up at the shop sign and noticed broken glass pane in the door. *Booth said it was personal*, he thought. *Holmes was his mother's maiden name. I wonder.*

Within seconds, smoke poured out from the broken window ending his contemplation.

"Fire," he screamed spitting out dirt. "Sound the alarm. Fire!" Avers had no idea where the nearest alarm could be but he knew someone in the neighborhood would.

A few people ambled out of the homes to watch the fire. Avers could feel a western wind brush against his hair as if to tempt the fire to burn.

Local residents filled the street within moments. Avers stood back among other spectators. Some were still in night clothes. Most were fully dressed. He was almost amused how people were entertained by the fire. He could understand their morbid fascination. He helplessly looked on as the entire storefront burst into flames. The hanging sign dropped onto the wooden sidewalk and enveloped in flames.

The clanging of bells could be heard coming up the street. A horse-drawn steamer pulled up to the fire and people scattered to make way. Avers could see the name, Little Giant, painted on the brass and nickel-plated tank. Powered by a steam engine mounted on the back of the wagon, the cylindrical tank looked like gigantic well-used milk pail. Little Giant was Chicago's oldest steam engine still in service.

Avers judged the galloping draft horses to be Percheron, approximately 1400 sturdy pounds each. Fire horses had to be strong, obedient and fearless. Well-trained, they were sometimes required to wait while men fought a blaze even if flames surrounded them.

Fire fighters hopped off the wagon and unhitched the horses to get them away from the flying sparks. The wind now shifted from the south west pushing fiery torrents across the buildings. Flames spread to three-quarters of the block.

Another group of fire fighters attached a hose to the nearest fireplug. Avers took a closer look at the hydrant. Oddly enough, it was constructed of wood and shaped like a butter churn.

"Start the pump," yelled one of the men.

In order to create enough steam to force the pump into action, a stoker shoveled wood or coal into the boiler tank. Pipemen attached an intake valve to the hydrant to blast water out two hoses. Avers watched the fire brigade perform this maneuver with practiced ease.

Gallons of water poured out of the hoses onto the fire.

The wind doubled as another fire steamer, Chicago, arrived from the south. It positioned itself north of the fire. At its back hung a brass and cut-glass carriage lamp with the number 5 etched in it. Little Giant had one too but the number 6 was engraved on that one.

Again Avers watched one group guided the horse away from the flames and another hooked hoses to a fire hydrant. This time a hose sprung several leaks.

Flames had already spread to a couple lumber yards with coal piles.

People dragged out their household items like clothes, beds, and other pieces of furniture to stack them into the middle of the street to save them.

Avers went up to a man who appeared to be in charge.

"I'm Lt. Avers U.S. Army, sir. Anything I can do to help?" Culver felt some responsibility because he again was unable to apprehend Booth.

"Sound a second alarm!" Third Assistant Marshal Matthias Benner shouted ignoring Avers.

"Where is it?"

Annoyed Benner shoved Avers aside. "My men will take care of it.

Please just stay out of the way!"

Avers understood. But he prepared himself for any opportunity to help.

The wind carried cinders and flames afloat causing the buildings on the other side of Canal Street to start burning. The second steamer had finally replaced its hose and began putting out those flames. Avers moved further north with the crowd.

The fires trailed them. Avers stood watching another block engulfed in flames as more steamers and even a hose elevator pulled up to douse the flames. More fire officials showed up as Avers watched Benner relinquish jurisdiction.

A six-foot tall man with a spade beard and moustache took command of the situation. He wore a narrow peaked cap and a long-belted coat with brass buttons in spite of the radiating heat.

He ordered a group of men to stall the fire by tearing down fences and wooden shacks as well as uprooting the sidewalks. He directed steamers and hose carts to encircle the fire. The dirt in the street became muddy.

Unable to stand by passively any longer, Avers charged forth and as-sisted with the organized destruction. He grabbed an axe from a fire en-gine to hack away at anything wooden and unburned mere feet away from the flames.

A loud cracking noise reverberated throughout the street and stopped everyone in their action. A building collapsed and the blaze shot out into the middle of the street. The furniture thought to be safe caught fire. The Chicago was surrounded in flames. Instinctively, the men ran for their lives.

Recovering after a moment, they rushed back. Avers dropped the axe and joined them in the struggle to drag the steamer out of danger. Like a stubborn mule, the steamer refused to budge, and then it relented. Slow, at first, with flames creeping closer and closer to the men. They continued to roll it north. The men built up enough speed to turn it toward the Chicago River near a tall structure. The men hooked up the hose to another hy-drant.

"Douse the National Elevator! Keep it from burning!" ordered Benner.

Avers watched the men water down the tall structure. Its tower reached into the night sky. Avers ran back and retrieved the axe he dropped.

He heard a group of men shout for help. They were milling about by the railroad tracks. He ran to them. Railroad tracks traversed the east side of Canal Street.

"The passenger cars are in the path of the fire," said one man.

"We've got to tear down that shed near the depot," yelled another.

Actually in unintended unison, the volunteers pushed and hacked at the shed until it finally crashed to the ground. Shoveling the debris away from the railway cars, the fire had no way to spread there despite the increasing wind.

Avers and the other men then physically pushed the rolling stock away from the growing inferno preventing more fuel for the fire. One, two, three, four cars were heaved north along the tracks safe from the fire.

Avers and seven other men saw a lumberyard just south of their position burst into flames. They ran toward the flames. The lumberyard was next to the river so they used whatever was handy to push the piles of lumber into the river. The men rammed hand carts, wheel barrows, and horse wagons to bang into the stacks of posts, beams, and boards to knock them into the river. After about the fifth stack rolled over the edge into the water they realized they were trapped by fire in the middle of the yard. The gate they entered was now a wall of flame. Surrounded by the blaze, the air thickened with smoke and stench of burned wood. Broiling heat pressed against them.

The slimy Chicago River presented their only escape option. Despite the blistering heat from the fire, the river water would be numbingly frigid. The volunteers faced a choice of being burned alive or possibly drowning while cold.

Avers stared over the edge and realized all the lumber floating.

"Hey, look. We can use the wood to float on top of the water," he shouted.

"Shove that last stack and we'll jump in with it!"

"Excellent idea," agreed one of the men and they put their shoulders against it.

"One, two three, heave!"

The stack tumbled down and slid along the bank of the river and splashed into the water. The eight men rode planks like sleds down a snowy hill. They whooped and hollered. Hitting the cold water at top speed did little more than to invigorate them as they paddled north on their makeshift rafts with the current.

By now, the Chicago Police Department blocked off a bridge at Adams Street to stop more onlookers from clogging the streets. Avers couldn't believe his eyes as several horse-drawn carriages approached with even more sight-seers.

Yet another steamer, called the Titsworth, pulled up next to the bridge. Using the hoses, police and fire men pulled the volunteers up from the river.

Avers could see the hair on the firemen and horses was singed. The Titsworth was there to spray water on the street and buildings north of the fire to impede the progress of the fire. The steamer and its men were successful in their efforts.

Avers could see sailors climb the riggings on the ships on the river to get a better view. Horse carriages stopped by the police merely rode north to the next bridge over. Fortunately, the Madison Street Bridge was built two blocks further away so floating embers died out before they could do harm.

Avers focused his attention elsewhere. He joined the damp volunteers as they rebounded. Undaunted, they trampled back to the fire to assist further.

The fire engulfed four neighborhood blocks now.

The volunteers moved in unison west along Adams Street. Avers was now accepted as one of them so he went with the flow.

They proceeded one block to Clinton Street and proceeded south to see where they could assist without getting in the way. Several fire officials nodded in recognition but waved them further south.

Across from the fire, Avers glimpsed a throng of people standing on a shed to watch the action. More and more people climbed on top. The darkness from the night made it difficult to count how many were there. Avers watched as the shed quivered each time someone new crawled on top.

Avers tapped the shoulder of the volunteer in front of him and pointed.

"Hold it, men," he shouted. The group froze and looked at the shed just across the street from where the fire started. The shed swayed in the wind.

No police were in sight so the volunteers screamed.

"Get down from there!"

"Go back!"

"Get off the roof!"

They waved their hands to get the attention of the mob but it was no use.

Avers took a quick count of thirty people, but more than three times as many stood and watched mesmerized by the flames and water and smoke.

Finally as if on cue, the shed groaned, creaked, and fell to the ground. The sidewalk next to it collapsed as well. Volunteers ran to the rescue.

Avers heard a man screaming from the boarding house on the other side of the street. Although the fire just started, the smoke enveloped the building.

"Help! I can't see anything!" a voice from above called out.

Seeing the injured were being pulled from the shed collapse, Avers ran across the street.

Noting that the man was on the third floor, he crashed through the front door and hurried up the stairs. Holding his wet shirt over his mouth, he was able to locate the man who stumbled into the third floor hallway. The man was shoeless and the heat burned his hair and whiskers.

The smoke stung Avers' eyes but he was able to quickly lead the man to the stairs and down to the street.

Outside the burning building, Avers asked, "Is there anyone else in the building?"

"No, I'm the last one." The man coughed

"Last one?"

"Yes, everyone else was evicted yesterday."

"And you stayed?"

"Yes. Now I have to leave!" he said angrily as he stormed off without a further word to Avers.

Avers followed the man to a saloon. It was the same bar he ducked into earlier that night when following Booth.

"Drinks are on the house," the bartender shouted as they walked in the door. The shoeless man walked up to the bar and started drinking.

The bartender handed out cigars with every drink. Avers watched amazed as the patrons sat calmly while fiery chaos was going on outside. The southern walls started to smolder from the intense heat being fanned by the wind. A small flame appeared in the middle of the wall. Some of the patrons put down their drinks and lugged out some copper tanks about two feet long with hoses attached. These portable fire extinguishers hissed a spray of a white foam solution to the wall. As the smoke dissipated, they resumed their drinking.

Suddenly aware how parched the fire had made him, Avers enjoyed a free beverage and admired at the ingenuity of the bartender. He had his own personal volunteer fire department.

Occasionally, a member of the Chicago Fire Department would stop in to quench his thirst. After a quick gulp, he returned to his duty, fighting the blaze.

Avers left the comfort of the saloon and once again breached the fire outside. Hoses lined the streets. Men were as close as twenty feet fighting the flames.

He helped drag ruined hoses out of the way from the firemen. The blaze battered other fire equipment as well. One steamer was damaged. Its wheels burned off while on Canal Street. The intense heat dented and cracked the steamer itself. A hose cart was swept away in flames when its

" DRINKS ARE ON THE HOUSE. "

fire hose burned.

Avers rejoined his fellow volunteers as they ripped down buildings and fences to establish fire breaks, successfully preventing the spread of the blaze.

As the night wore on, his muscles ached. His eyes were red and swollen. His clothes were both wet and charred. The stench of burnt wood and smoke covered his body. He daren't complain. Everyone else fighting the fire that Booth started was in the same condition.

Avers saw a young man in a dark suit and tie with a camera. He placed it on a three-foot black steamer trunk to take photographs of the blaze.

"How about helping?" Avers said with his voice croaking.

"I'm with the Daily Tribune," said the young man as he stuck out his hand. "Richard F. Cromie, professional journalist. And I leave fire fighting to the professionals. I report their bravery and skill to the public. That's my racket."

Avers couldn't resist but shake the hand of the reporter with a wooden camera.

"I'm surprised these buildings went up so fast. Some of them are made of steel and brick," Avers said.

Richard F. Cromie laughed. Avers looked at the man.

"Like we say at the Tribune, they're 'firetraps pleasing to the eyes.' The façade is made of steel and iron and brick. The store fronts only. And the much-touted Athens marble is sometimes limestone from Athens, Illinois."

"Why waste money on that?"

"To appeal to customers. Cheaper, but no safer. Especially in this area. 'The Red Flash' district—insurance companies call this. That's their racket. Nothing but factories, lumber yards, a timber depot here and a paper box company to boot. Add a few shacks that they call a boarding house. Not to mention saloons on every corner."

"Saloons?"

"Alcohol burns doesn't it?"

"I just saw men inside that bar over there keeping from it going up in flames with their extinguishers!"

"Good old Daniel Quirk! What a racket he's got going. Those booze hounds will stay and drink all night to keep that place from burning down."

"Aren't there any more crews to help?"

"You're looking at it, boy," Richard F. Cromie said and turned away to take a photograph.

"You seem to know a lot about this area," Avers said as he grabbed his axe.

"This area? I know this whole damn town, man," Cromie boasted as he slid a glass plate out of the side of the camera and carefully placed it inside a velvet bag. He grabbed another plate and slid it into the back of the camera. He wiped off the lens. A quick nod and a smile to Avers and Cromie moved further east for another angle of the action.

Avers rejoined the firemen and volunteers. They continued throughout the night. Demolishing buildings and tearing up sidewalks. On occasion they poured a handy water bucket on any nearby flame. They helped in containing the fire to the four block area.

At some point, the volunteers and the fire department acted like machines. Performing the same movement over and over and merely shifting positions. No one was left to rescue.

As the night wore on and the flames diminished so did the crowds.

At dawn, Chief Fire Marshall Robert Williams, the six-foot tall man with a spade beard and moustache, departed for breakfast and left Benner in charge again to put out any remaining fires.

Avers was invited to join the volunteers for drinks but he declined. His scorched shirt and pants were completely dry now. Like the other volunteers and fire fighters, his skin was reddened and slightly burned. Cinders made all their eyes bloodshot and swollen.

He surveyed that area. Steamer No. 3 was in shambles. A hose cart was still smoldering. Personal belongings pulled into the middle of the street to be safe from fire were now piles of blackened rubbish.

Exhausted, Avers sat down on one of the remaining planked sidewalks across from Quirk's saloon and closed his eyes.

CHAPTER 5

He might have slept for a few seconds, a few minutes, or a few hours. He didn't know. But he did know the voice that woke him up.

"Shit, look at this shit," a voice with a subtle Southern accent spoke behind him.

"It did enough damage," said the voice, deeper but same Southern accent.

Avers' swollen eyes forced themselves open; daylight exposed a devastated area. Few companies of fire fighters were still watering down any spontaneous bonfire no matter its size.

Avers was still sitting on the side of a wooden sidewalk scorched but not burned. He didn't need to turn his head to know they were the two men from the night before. They were part of a much smaller crowd gathered to gawk at the sprinkling among the dying embers.

Down the street, Avers heard a man cry as he learned that his wife died in the fire in their home.

The tall man and medium-sized man wormed their way to the back of the crowd. Avers listened to their footsteps on the sidewalk go off into the distance.

Refreshed from the nap, Avers found renewed strength to track them. He had to find out more of this retaliation they planned. He stood up and saw them hesitate at a corner. He still stank of smoke. It clung to him. People moved out of his way. Their nose wrinkling as he passed them. He didn't want to lose sight of the two men who lingered for a bit then rounded the corner.

He followed them for a few blocks giving them a lead of about half a city block. Curiosity seekers littered the roadway and walkway. Avers leaned against a telegraph pole or hid inside a doorway so the two men wouldn't detect him.

In a few blocks, they were back in Conley's Patch. The two men paused at the end of an alley. Then the men ducked inside the back of a rickety shack with their saddled dark brown horses tied to a hitching post.

Slowly Avers quietly trod close to the gray-brown shanty. The windows were shuttered so he couldn't hear or see anything. He crept closer but still couldn't hear anything or anyone inside. He inched next to the door.

The door flew open and Booth looked at Avers.

"It took you long enough to get here, sir," he said welcomingly and waved him inside.

Avers entered and realized the three men were waiting for him.

"My good sir, I am glad you accepted our understated invitation," Booth grinned.

"Invitation?" Avers' voice cracked.

"Shit, we saw you helping put out that fire last night," the medium-sized man said.

"I even saw you fall into the river," said the tall man. "Have a nice swim, yankee?"

Booth closed the door behind Avers. "I thought it was a valiant but futile effort."

Booth pulled up a chair for Avers and invited him to sit down with a wave of his right hand. His thumb looking very distorted with the gesture.

"We took turns keeping an eye on you, shithead. We took turns sleeping," said the medium-sized man.

"Once we saw you sleeping, it was easy to wake you up and let you follow us here," the tall man said as he walked behind Avers.

Avers realized they had surrounded him in the chair. The clothes on the two men were rumpled. Booth's appearance, however, remained polished as ever. He still wore a sable frock coat and felt derby but now sported a dark blue suit with black bow tie.

The nap refreshed Avers and his eyes were clearer but he was still weakened from hunger and the labors of the previous night. The three men had a simple task to tie Avers into the chair.

"We didn't want to leave any loose ends, as it were," Booth said.

"Loose ends?"

"Yes, my good man. You, sir, are a loose end. We need to avoid any loose ends especially loose ends from last night. Last night, you see, was merely a prelude. You see, a greater spectacle is planned for tonight."

"And your dead body will be among many," laughed the tall man.

"So, what you plan to set another neighborhood in Chicago on fire?"

"Not merely a neighborhood, the whole town. The burning of Chicago! That task falls on my shoulders," bragged Booth.

"I'm gonna set Springfield on fire," said the medium man.

"And I'm leaving shortly for Urbana," said the tall man.

"I have been mapping out various sites. I've acquainted myself with firebox locations and how to counter them. Tonight, the Ku Klux Klan shall recreate Sherman's March to the Sea, his burning of Atlanta, only it will be a march surrounding the Great Lakes. Klan members are stationed north in a town in Wisconsin called Peshtigo and three more towns in Michigan, Holland, Port Huron, and Manistee," Booth evangelized and held up a sheet of paper.

"I have confirmed that my comrade-in-arms are, indeed, in place to enact the Klan's magnificent display of power tonight. Tonight along with Chicago, Springfield and Urbana, they will burn. As retribution for all this harassment from government politicians and subversive newspapers," Booth pontificated with a demonic gleam in his eyes.

"Calling us vigilantes instead of patriots!"

"Persecuting us. Suppressing our right to freely assemble while calling darkies free men!"

"We've got members of our fraternity placed in each one of those towns.

Tonight those six towns and Chicago will light the skies!"

"What?" puffed out Avers.

"Our comrades, our brother in arms, will start fires in each of those towns in reprisal for the abominations the North has inflicted on the South!"

The tall man wrapped a gag around Avers' mouth.

"I'm gonna start downtown Urbana on fire and spread it out from there!" laughed the tall man.

The medium-sized man was not about to be out-done. "Springfield, the state capital where Lincoln is buried. I'm gonna enjoy torching that place. I'm gonna start with Lincoln's lawyer's office and work my way from there."

Booth allowed for a dramatic pause. He placed his fist on his hip and raised his index finger in the air.

"I've decided to ignite that low-life Irish ghetto along De Koven. Filled with human trash, so-called immigrants, contaminating our great land. And then that damned Catholic Church St. Paul's will be next. After I remove its foreign influence, I'll work my way north. From what we observed last night, the accursed fire department is limited to handling one conflagration. But we'll see how they fare against multiple pyres of glory. Pyres devoted to cleansing this city of its foreign disease, its corruption. My mission will finally culminate with reducing Proclamation 95 to ashes and burning out the spawn of the greatest traitor America has ever known! Not only this town, but those other Midwestern towns shall be purged for the glory of our country. It is our patriotic duty!"

The two men with tears in their eyes almost broke in applause at Booth's soliloquy.

When Booth was about to take a bow, the medium-sized man cleared his throat.

"What the hell is Proclamation 95?"

"Let us coordinate our watches," Booth said shrugging off his comrade's limited knowledge.

All three men pulled out open-faced pocket watches and compared them. The medium-sized man twisted the stem to match the time on the other two.

"It was decided that the reckoning, perdition, shall begin at 8:30 p.m. tonight." Booth smirked with a wink to Avers as if that time should have special significance to him.

"Gentlemen, it is time to part company. We plan to meet in South Carolina in one week to receive our well-deserved accolades. Gentlemen shall think themselves accurs'd they were not here, and hold their man-hood cheap!"

The three men shook hands.

"Stop your squirming, yankee," the medium-sized man said to Avers. "You ain't gonna git comfortable in that there chair."

Booth faced the other men.

"How long will it take you to get to Springfield?"

"Just a couple of hours!"

"To Urbana?"

"Most of the day if I leave now."

"Then leave now," Booth instructed.

The tall man headed out the door and hopped on his horse. The sounds of hooves galloping away receded quickly in the distance.

"Kill him after I leave," Booth said dismissively. "Leave his body here. The fire will cover it up. I have a few more arrangements to make. And I do so abhor the sight of blood. Sic Semper Chicago!"

Booth bowed deeply as if he was taking a curtain call. Doffing his hat, he stepped through the door. He hesitated and winked at Avers. Tapping his derby, Booth smiled and said, "There's a very real chance that your body will be incinerated to nothingness tonight."

He left with amused thoughts that the corpse of his hapless captive would burn alongside Irish and German immigrant scum nearby.

The medium-sized man grinned and walked to the lop-sided bed. It was little more than loosely assembled boards and stained blankets. He pulled out a pistol from underneath the rolled-up sheet that pretended to be a pillow on a thin, ripped mattress.

CHAPTER 6

"I should just leave you here to burn," he said. Pointing the gun at Avers' head, he whispered, "Bang."

While the Klan members were bragging about their plot, Avers slipped his knife from the side of his belt into his right hand. While they thought he was wiggling to get comfortable, he actually sliced part of the rope.

The medium-sized man aimed the gun and said, "Shit, I should leave you here to burn, but I won't."

I've been beaten three times. Now it is my turn, thought Avers. With a quick, practiced flick, Avers threw the knife directly into the man's throat.

"Shit," gasped the wounded man.

In the few remaining moments of his life, he pulled the trigger. The shot went wild and the gun dropped to the floor.

Hearing the shot a block away, Booth smiled.

Avers leaped from the chair and plunged the knife deeper into the killer's throat until no sign of life remained. He ripped off the gag and spat.

"Springfield's more than a couple hours ride, you stupid bastard. That's just another one of your stupid mistakes. It's obvious none of you ever served in the Army. Otherwise, you would have searched for my knife."

Avers picked up the dead man and placed him in the bed. He covered him with the least stained blanket. Picking up the gun, he smiled that it was an 1860 Colt Army revolver. He broke it open and emptied its three remaining bullets into his hand. He slipped the bullets into his pocket, shoved the revolver into the back of his trousers, and left the shack.

Avers judged the breed of the remaining horse to be a Morgan. He preferred them because they were friendly and adaptable. He hopped on what he assumed (from the process of elimination) was the dead man's horse and rode it a little more than a mile north to the Tremont House where he was staying. He paused briefly on the Adams Street Bridge to toss the revolver into the river.

A five-story luxury hotel, the Tremont House, started as two smaller hotels that ironically were destroyed by a fire. Its tin-covered roof was designed for fire protection. The hotel boasted to be the first one of its kind to be lit with gas in Chicago. Its balcony hosted a speech by Lincoln followed by one by Stephen Douglas the following night in 1858. In fact, poet Ralph Waldo Emerson stayed there during his lecture tour that same year.

Accommodations at the southwest corner of Dearborn and Lake Streets included a dining room, indoor plumbing, barber shop, apothecary, laundry, and a small livery in back. It was located a few blocks of the Union Depot.

Avers tied up his horse in the back stable of the hotel. After a momentary talk with the liveryman, he walked around to the front. The main entrance was on the west side of Dearborn.

At first, O'Hara the doorman stopped the dirty, smelly man with spots of blood on his shirt from entering the lobby. Avers realized the sight he made.

"I'm a guest of Mrs. Lincoln! The name's Philip Avers."

"Saints preserve us! Please, sir, the other guests," the doorman whispered with a thick Irish brogue.

Looking at his hands, Avers relented, "I see your point."

"I'll have one of the boys meet you by the kitchen door."

Avers retreated to the rear entrance. The doorman directed one the bell-hops to meet Avers and discreetly escort him to his room. Taking the staff staircase, they ascended unnoticed by other guests. When the hallway was clear, Avers snuck to his hotel. Upon entering the room, he dropped a coin into the bellhop's waiting hand and shut the door. He tossed his knife on the floor. He toppled in the bed and slept immediately. Exhaustion took over.

CHAPTER 7

Avers awoke by 1 p.m. His muscles were stiff after so much exertion. He stumbled to the private bath at the end of the hall. He peeled off the soot-covered, smoke-reeked clothes off his body. He washed himself and felt good to be rid of the grime and soot.

Back in his room, he donned clean black cotton trousers, a white shirt and black vest. He slipped into his polished black boots. He transferred the three bullets into his money belt. The knife was slid in a specially-designed sheath in his shirt sleeve. He decided against a tie today but buttoned his collar. He left the brown clothes from last night to whatever the maid would do with them. He grabbed his gambler's hat but decided not to wear it. He jogged down the stairs to the hotel's barber shop. His singed hair was trimmed and chin stubble and the grubby moustache were shaved off.

O'Hara nodded approvingly as Avers made his way through the lobby to the dining room.

Avers was able to order before lunch officially ended. Realizing he hadn't eaten since the night before, he consumed a grand meal of steak and pota-toes. He enjoyed coffee with the meal. He needed a clear head for tonight.

As he ate, he wrote out the details of the conspiracy plans that Booth had bragged about. He listed the targeted cities of Chicago, Peshtigo, Urbana, Holland, Port Huron, and Manistee. Springfield was omitted be-cause it was safe for tonight at least. He also wrote a letter to Mary Lincoln to update her on his progress of bringing Tad's murderer to justice. She was staying with a friend who lived just west of Chicago.

He enjoyed a final cup of coffee as he finished his notes and sealed them in an envelope. He paid his bill and left.

Avers entrusted the letter for Mary Lincoln to a desk clerk. Tucking his notes into his vest pocket, he forgot about his hat, and exited out to Dearborn Street with a quick nod to the doorman.

"Looking quite the gentleman, sir," O'Hara said pleased at how Avers cleaned up from this morning.

"Thank you," Avers replied with a wink.

Enjoying the warm autumn weather, he briskly walked the five blocks to Lt. General Philip H. Sheridan's Army headquarters, stationed in the Merchant's Insurance Building.

Sheridan accepted the military command of the Military Division of the Missouri two years previously. With that post, the forty-year-old Civil War hero relocated its headquarters from St. Louis to Chicago and made his residence there.

Avers knew he had to warn authorities of the impending threat by the Klan. He realized local law enforcement wouldn't give any credence to him or his tidings of doom. Nor would the Chicago Fire Department. The mayor's office would disregard him as well. None of them would even consider warning the other towns if they did listen to him.

His recent encounter concerning the plot to drag America into the Franco-Prussian War provided him with some credibility with military intelligence. Although his persistence that Booth was alive still caused some concern of his mental stability. He knew a very good chance one of his contacts would get the warning into Sheridan's hands.

Also, Sheridan had the facilities to disperse these dire warnings to the proper authorities. Sheridan's position allowed him unlimited access to telegraphs.

Avers arrived at the Army Headquarters. But he was stopped by two armed guards before he could enter the building.

"Philip Avers with vital information for General Sheridan," Avers said saluting.

"Sir, you may not enter," responded the young private with the beginnings of a moustache on his upper lip.

"At least, get word to Lt. Col. William Campbell. We served together."

The young private nodded to the other guard, who dashed off.

Waiting for the response, Avers looked across LaSalle Street at the Courthouse. He admired the impressive ornamental cupola atop five stories of government offices. Its bell tolled four times. The Courthouse occupied the center of an entire city block. It towered over the square's landscape of trees and shrubs. It appeared as if it were in the middle of a country park rather than in the city business district.

An iron picket fence bordered the Courthouse Square filled with oak and elms trees. Between the trees ran sidewalks diagonally from the main entrance to the LaSalle and Clark corners

Within minutes, the young private accompanied an older distinguished looking officer.

Upon seeing Avers, Lt. Col. William Campbell's face broke out in a wide grin.

"You, ugly bastard, how are you?" he said shaking Avers' hand.

"Better than you, you sorry-looking swamp rat!"

They stepped outside into the bustling street. Non-descript people passed them. Horse-drawn carriages clopped through the intersection.

"You know I can't let you in without an official invite, Phil."

"I know. And I'm not looking for any favors. I've uncovered some vital information."

"How reliable?"

"I just want to let you know I confirmed the information you gave me. Klan members are in Chicago. In fact, here's a detailed report on their current locations and suspected plans. Sheridan needs to be alerted."

Avers handed over the envelope.

"The commander is at the Headquarters at Camp Highwood thirty miles away. I'll take a look."

"Sheridan needs to see it as soon as possible, Bill."

"Okay, I'll forward them on."

"This information is time sensitive. Plans are imminent. Some retaliation for Sherman's March to the Sea. Within twenty-four hours. Possibly as soon as tonight, if the information is reliable."

"Sounds a little fishy, Phil. But some sources have alluded to something was in the works. Confirmed?"

"I heard it directly from ..."

"Don't say it. Don't even whisper the name. That's why you insist..."

Campbell frowned at Avers' near slip of the tongue.

"Bill, you know it's true."

"No, I don't. I wish you'd accept that."

"I wish I could too. But I saw him."

Campbell sighed deeply at his poor deluded friend.

Avers had grown accustomed to this reaction. He would have been surprised if his friend had not done that.

"I'll see what I can do," Campbell promised.

The old comrades shook hands and parted company.

Avers wasn't surprised that he was denied permission to meet with General Sheridan personally even if the general was in his fourth-floor office overlooking Washington Street. The armed guard heavily suggested that Sheridan was in the building. It was easier for Campbell to deny it and dissuade his friend. But at least, the letter would make its way into his hands. He had enough influence for that. His old army pal would see to that. The old army pal felt sorry for Avers. Campbell was the officer who had to accept Avers' resigned commission from the Army.

Avers hiked back to the hotel confident Sheridan would receive the warning. Whether Sheridan would receive it in time or act quickly on it, he didn't know.

With the U.S. Army forewarned, any obligation he felt to them was met. Now he needed to focus and prepare for the evening. The imminent capture of Booth was at hand.

CHAPTER 8

On his walk back to the Tremont House, Avers thought about the fact he no longer possessed his saber from his time in the U.S. Army. He missed it but his military training drilled in that he would never be without his knife. He patted his wrist to make sure it was still available. But he knew he needed more.

He returned to the Tremont House. He strode up the stairs barely touching the banisters.

Once inside his room, he located his Army Colt revolver and checked the cylinders. Five chambers were filled. He didn't load a live round in the firing chamber. While in the Army, he once saw a gun go off in a soldier's holster because he had all the chambers filled.

He donned a dark corduroy blazer. The revolver fit perfectly in the blazer's inside pocket. He felt the side arm's weight of almost three pounds rest against his chest. Before venturing out into the balmy autumn evening, Avers lingered over another meal of steak, potatoes, and coffee. During his meal, he read an article in the Tribune about the fire the previous night.

Its editor Horace White wrote "For days past, alarm has followed alarm, but the comparatively trifling losses have familiarized us to the pealing of the Courthouse bell, and we have forgotten that the absence of rain for three weeks has left everything in so dry and inflammable condition that a spark might start a fire which would sweep from end to end of the city."

Avers shrugged at the journalistic hyperbole that newspapers were noted for. He finished his meal and put it on his hotel bill. Mary Lincoln promised to cover his expenses.

He sensed he probably wouldn't eat again until he captured Booth tonight. He knew where Booth would be at 8:30 p.m. tonight. He would place Booth under arrest and see him hang for his crimes.

The bell inside the hotel chimed 7 p.m. Now it was time to track down Booth. He asked the Irish doorman for directions to De Koven Street.

"Now, why would ye be wanting to go there?" O'Hara asked squinting one eye.

"That's no concern of yours, Mr. O'Hara," Avers replied with a smirk.

O'Hara winked and told him to ride west on Randolph and turn south on Canal, "a wee bit less than a mile."

Avers entered the livery and tipped the stable boy. He hopped on the dark brown saddle horse. He didn't follow O'Hara's directions. He made a side trip back to the shack in Conley's Patch. He confirmed that Booth hadn't returned because the body remained undisturbed. The element of surprise was still in his favor.

Avers' horse trotted over to Adams Street and across the bridge to Canal Street. He rode past the blocks ravaged by fire the night before. The ashes rekindled the stench of charred wood in his nostrils.

He rode along Canal Street south for almost a mile until a sign listing De Koven Street shown under a street light. The night sky darkened with just a hint of a sunset. He pivoted the horse east and rode a couple of blocks through the working-class neighborhood until De Koven ended. He neither saw nor heard any signs of life in the street in the dim light of the night. The lights in the homes were out and no sounds emanated from them.

He noticed the trees along De Koven. Being fall, no leaves occupied the branches, of course. The trunks appeared malnourished and thin. They grew in irregular places on either side of the sidewalks as if they were unplanned. One may be off by itself. Or a couple intertwined their branches.

He turned around and rode west. He trotted about a block and a half, past Clinton Street but halted the horse before Jefferson Street.

Avers heard what sounded like a party in a house. To call the dwelling a raised ranch would be generous. It was four wooden walls with a pitched roof resting on top. The loud laughter and three thick Irish brogues came from behind the house. A similar house was behind it and a bit off to the side. Further back, a flimsy stable with an open weather-beaten door attracted Avers' attention. Although the light inside was dim, in the darkness of the October night, it functioned like a beacon.

He tied the horse to a decrepit wooden picket fence in front of the shabby single-story frame shack. He didn't see any address number posted. He crept along the passageway on the side of the house. He heard movement inside. He passed the other house, another two-room shanty. It was silent.

Avers gained a better view of the barn about forty feet behind the second house. Its door was nailed opened on the right side of the barn. He quietly snuck across the yard closer to the door. He peeked inside to see Booth drinking with two Irish men in lambent light.

Like most other Chicagoans, the men wore dark brown clothes and sported thick moustaches. Two wore derbies and one was bare-headed. One of the derbied men was Booth, dressed also in brown but nattily. They all sat around a crate turned on its side. Three bottles, one empty, surrounded an oil lamp in the middle of the makeshift tabletop. The brass-based lamp with its glass globe and chimney allowed its flame to light up the entire inside of the barn.

Avers considered this drinking scene odd considering how Booth cursed the Irish "trash" earlier that day. Now Booth was pouring drinks and buddying around with two of them. They sat on stools among several cows and a calf. Two dark-colored horses were secured outside the barn. The brown one was saddled. The other tied to a wagon.

Avers drew his revolver as he watched them imbibe. They held mason jars substituting for drinking cups and were heartily laughing.

Booth, being an actor, could affect a phony Irish brogue. Again he was ingratiating himself with his newfound drinking buddies.

"Begosh and begorrah, are ye certain they won't wake up?" Booth asked as he filled the mason jars.

"Tis true, they're heavy, heavy sleepers. The whole of the neighborhood is like that. The O'Learies, God bless them, they bed early so to wake up at the wee hours of the mornin' for the milking of the cows. Tis' true or my name isn't Dennis Regan," laughed the man.

"And you, Peg Leg Sullivan, what's your business here?" asked Booth.

Sullivan winced at the nickname.

"Did not mean to offend, Daniel," Booth said laying on the brogue very thick.

"It tis what it tis. As to my business, my sainted mother owns one of them there cows," belched Sullivan.

"...BOOTH DRINKING WITH TWO IRISH MEN..."

Annoyed by such lack of culture, Booth changed the subject.

"Saints preserve us, and how did you lose your leg, Daniel?" asked Booth as he poured more into the other man's cup.

"The War. Let me regale the powerful tale of how it happened as I fought off a dozen Rebs," Daniel said as he gulped his fill.

"Not that tall tale again," Dennis interrupted. "Mr. Sullivan here is well known for kissing the Blarney Stone."

"Mr. Regan, you should be talking about Blarney. Tis well known the fables that you tell," Daniel retorted drunkenly.

Booth casually pulled out the pocket watch. Eyeing the time, his demeanor changed dramatically.

"Well, I've had enough of both of your drivel. I didn't expect you buffoons here but it may be happenstance," Booth said standing up and dropping the brogue. He tossed his derby off to the side.

"Fill up the cups, boyo, and share us some of your lies," the man with the peg leg said pushing his cup toward Booth.

"I think you Micks have had quite enough for the night. You should go off and fondle your sheep or cows of whatever you scum like to molest at night," Booth sauntered over to a bale of hay against the east wall and emptied a full bottle of whiskey over it.

"Feck off," said Regan.

"Wasting that fine liquor like that. Tis a shame, it tis," Sullivan said as he tried to stand. Then he sat down again.

Again Booth assumed a dramatic pose with his fist above his head.

"You're part of the disgusting filth invading America. Contaminating America. I believe you and the rest of the immigrant rabble need to be cauterized!" Booth grabbed the kerosene lamps and shattered it against the hay where the whiskey was spilt. The hay smoldered for a moment then burst into small flames.

The two Irishmen just stared in drunken disbelief.

Booth grabbed the second bottle of whiskey to smash in the flames.

"If you tell anyone. Who would believe two Irish drunks?" sneered Booth.

Ignoring the two Irishmen to the right of him, Avers entered the barn and pointed the Colt on Booth.

"But what about a sober witness? Once again you're trapped in a burning barn."

Booth stared with his mouth open, momentarily stunned by Avers' presence.

"So the fool didn't kill you!"

"Springfield won't burn tonight."

"Stop waving that thing around, you eejit. It could go off," said Sullivan.

Booth ducked behind Sullivan. Avers' aim followed the assassin. Sullivan saw the long barrel point at him and jumped up. Booth threw the bottle up at Avers. Both Sullivan and Regan knocked Avers to the ground driving for the bottle. Having caught the bottle, Regan leaned against a post. Sullivan raised his fists trying to focus on Avers.

Avers' Colt spun to the dirt floor and bounced over to Booth. In one fluid motion, Booth grabbed the revolver and struck Regan behind the ear knocking his derby off. Regan fell over.

The bottle broke and whiskey spilled out.

"What ja do that fer, boyo?" Sullivan said as he staggered to Booth. Booth pistol whipped Sullivan as Avers struggled to his feet.

The fire quickly spread throughout the bales of hay and toward the spilled whiskey. The heat intensified.

Pointing the gun at Avers, Booth backed toward the open barn door.

"A dilemma for a fool. Save these dregs of society or die trying to capture me," Booth mocked and sidled out the door. Avers listened to the sound of a galloping horse thumping away in the alley. Flames shot up the side toward the loft filled with hay.

Without hesitation, Avers pulled Regan through the open door clear of the burning whiskey. He ran to the alley. He caught a glimpse of Booth riding to Clinton Street and turning south. Then he returned to the burning barn and lugged Sullivan to safety. The fresh air revived Sullivan quickly.

Disregarding Avers, Sullivan screamed, "Fire! Fire! Fire! Holy Mother of God! Get help!" Then he limped back to rescue the animals.

Avers watched the fire run across the dry grass onto the tall rustic fence and clapboard shed next door. The next door house was directly in the path.

Regan pounded on the back door to wake the O'Leary family.

"Patrick! Patrick O'Leary! Wake up! Wake up, man!"

Bleary-eyed, Patrick O'Leary opened the door. Ignoring Regan, the blaze was the only thing he saw.

Patrick yelled, "Kate! The barn is afire!"

Running past Regan to De Koven Street, Avers felt the wind pick up from the south as if to urge the fire northeast.

CHAPTER 9

Confident that the fire would be attended to, Avers untied and bounded onto his horse in one fluid motion.

Following in pursuit, Avers arrived at the corner of De Koven and Clinton in time to see Booth turn east a couple blocks ahead. He raced his horse south.

Rounding the corner, Avers galloped in the direction he saw Booth ride. He saw no one. He slowed to a trot. He came to a two-story white frame building with a fire alarm call box on the side.

Avers realized that pulling the alarm took priority over capturing Booth. He slid off the horse next to the alarm. It was locked.

Bounding onto the sidewalk, he peered inside the shop windows under a wooden soffit. Thick black curtains behind the window displays and advertisements obstructed any view inside. He pounded on the front door under a sign that read, "Deutsche Apothecary." Whoever was inside safeguarded the key that unlocked the alarm. No one answered. He battered on the door some more. Still no response from inside.

Avers ran around the back and saw Booth's horse tied to a timber frame hitching post. The back door was slightly open and Avers tied his horse next to Booth's.

He quietly stepped inside. He entered a back room well-lit with several lamps on desks. The door was open so he could see into the other room.

Booth held a gun on a dark-haired clean shaven man in his twenties. Unlike so many Chicagoans Avers encountered, this man wore a white suit and a bow tie. Avers realized he must be the druggist of the apothecary.

"Give me the key," Booth demanded.

"Ach, you needn't have pointed zat gun at me," the man said with a German accent.

The man handed over the call box key to Booth.

"NO!" shouted Avers. Booth turned to the sound of Avers' voice.

"Come out with your hands up or I'll shoot him," Booth demanded.

Avers held his hands in front of him as he stepped from the back room and beside the drugstore counter. The shop was barren except for the counter and a few wall shelves behind it.

Booth's face perked up in recognition.

"We meet again. So glad you could join us, Mr...." Booth wrinkled his brow. "What is your name? We've never been formally introduced, sir."

"I'm ......"

"I don't care. I, of course, need no introduction," Booth waved him over with the gun. "Please come join Mr. Goll and myself,"

"Go make alarm. You have key," Goll said, shooing him away with both hands.

"That's the last thing he wants to do," Avers said, moving next to Goll.

"Alas, he's correct, you German fool. I want to make sure that fire spreads without interference from any fire brigade," laughed Booth.

Goll laughed. "It is you who are foolish, dumpkopf."

They heard someone run up the wooden sidewalk and knock on the front door.

"Not one word," warned Booth.

"Bruno, open the door. I need the key for alarm box," yelled the voice from the front door.

"That is William Lee, mine neighbor," whispered Goll. "He won't leave until he sees me."

"Get rid of him then. One note of warning and one of you dies," whispered Booth.

Goll raced to the front door and unlocked it. He opened it slightly.

"Vat is it, William? It is very late," Goll said annoyed.

"There's a fire. We need to pull the alarm. Where's the key?" Lee said desperately.

"No need. I saw fire truck pass just a few minutes ago," Goll responded calmly.

"Please, Bruno, the key!" begged Lee.

"No, alarm was sent. I told you fire truck passed by here already. Now go home and go to sleep, William!" Goll insisted as he slammed the door and locked it.

"You go to Hell, Bruno!" Lee swore as he ran off the sidewalk and back up the street.

"Very good!" said Booth.

"You, fool, the fire!" Avers said dejectedly.

"Ach! I do not want to get shot. And besides, this dummkopf!" Goll snickered.

"Sir, please speak English. You are in America after all," Booth said again pointing the gun at Goll's head.

"That call box is not important. It is not the only way the fire department will know of fire," Goll smiled.

"Is there another call box I missed?"

"Ja, but they see the fire from the Courthouse. They have lookout there on the roof. The fire department will alert closest fire house. Maybe a couple houses will burn but fire will be out soon enough, dummkopf!"

"I forgot about that! Where is this Courthouse? How far?" Booth placed the pistol against Goll's head.

"How far is the Courthouse from here?" Booth repeated pressing hard behind Goll's ear.

"A couple of miles northeast of here. Clark and Randolph," Goll gulped and closed his eyes.

Sensing Booth was distracted, Avers jumped toward him. Booth instinctively turned and shot. Avers collapsed.

Booth turned back and smashed the gun against Goll's temple. Goll dropped to the floor like a lead weight.

Booth sprinted out of the back of the store. He untied both horses and shooed Avers' away. He crawled onto his saddle horse and galloped northeast as fast as he could push the horse. Avers' horse instinctively returned to its last stable at the Tremont.

Blood dripped from Avers' unconscious form. Besides the blood, the only other movement in the room was an occasional twitch of Goll's arm.

CHAPTER 10

The time was 9:30 p.m. at the Courthouse in Chicago.

"You're standing on the fire watchman's platform surrounding the two-story of the Courthouse tower. Just this spring, we installed this clock. All four sides face all four directions, it does. The bell inside weighs five-and a half tons," Mathias Schaefer said proudly with a slight wiggle to his walrus moustache.

"The Courthouse itself is built in the very center of Chicago. If you look northwest, you can see the Water Tower. Built just two years ago with medieval turrets and arrow slits for decoration. Pulls water directly from Lake Michigan to one hundred and fifty-four miles of pipes under the entire city. It pumps water to hydrants for this whole section and stops baby fish from swimming into kitchen sinks."

Schaefer, a forty-year-old watchman and veteran of the fire department, was giving an impromptu tour to a very interested visitor. The brown haired, mustached, well-dressed man continued to ask a variety of questions. The man charmed a tour and seemed most interested in the area north of the tower.

To ease his boredom, Schaefer eagerly agreed to this spontaneous tour of the Courthouse cupola. Like other members of the Chicago Fire Department, he never missed a chance to show off the city's fire fighting expertise. So visitors and tours were not uncommon and very welcomed.

"Looks like something burning in the south," Schaefer paused.

"That's probably the fires from last night. Wasn't it out that way?"

"Of course. Of course. Among our newest fire engines, one's capable of pumping 700 gallons of water a minute and another with 900 gallons a minute."

Schaefer started to continue his tour on the east side. But the flames shooting in the sky in the south attracted Schaefer's attention again.

"No, son, that's a new fire. It'll be a thrill for you to see the fire department in action firsthand. First, I must notify my assistant." Schaefer put his spyglass to his eye to confirm his suspicions and identify the exact location of tonight's fire.

Booth pulled out the Colt and held it behind Schaefer's ear.

"Tell him to strike an alarm further away."

Schaefer eased the spyglass away from his eye. He turned his head. The gun barrel now pointed the center of his forehead. He focused on at the revolver's long barrel and gulped. He recognized it as an Army revolver.

Both of them walked over to the speaking tube connected to the lower level of the Courthouse.

Schaefer whistled to get the fire alarm operator's attention.

"Strike Box 342" he croaked into the tube.

"Where's that?" demanded Booth.

"A mile away. Canalport and Halsted," said Schaefer as he pointed southwest.

The fire telegraph operator acknowledged the call.

Booth struck Schaefer with the revolver. As Schaefer fell to the roof, Booth left. He ran down the iron stairway to the third floor looking for Schaefer's assistant.

Having issued the fire alarm, William J. Brown, the fire alarm/telegraph operator, continued playing his guitar to entertain his sixteen-year-old sister Sarah and her friend Maggie. His sister brought him supper because he had to work late.

Seeing Booth and his gun burst through the door, Brown heroically stood between the gunman and the two young ladies.

Lying on his back, Schaefer's eyes flickered open. Getting to his feet, Schaefer glared out into the hazy, moonless night lit up by the south side fire. He shook his head to recover and staggered to the speaking tube to warn Brown of the madman.

"I made a mistake, Brown. There's a fool with a gun. He forced me. Strike Box 319. Do it now!"

"No, Mathias."

"Boy, do what I tell you!"

"No, a second alarm would only create more confusion, Mathias," William said desperately.

Schaefer leaned his head against the wall in defeat.

"You're not alone are you, William?"

The long pause gave Schaefer his answer.

"He's got a gun on you, boy, doesn't he?"

Again silence.

"Your sister and her little friend are they still there?"

Still silence at the other end.

"Are they in any danger?"

"Not as long I don't send the second alarm," Brown said weakly.

"Damn him," Schaefer groaned.

Schaefer scurried to the stairs, through a pile of wood shavings, and dashed down two stories to the third floor.

Hearing the thunderous tread come down the stairs, Booth shifted to the doorway and waited. Schaefer burst through the door. Once again Booth clobbered him with the gun. Schaefer crumpled to the floor. A drop of blood trickled from his head wound to the hard wood flooring.

With Booth distracted, Brown nudged the girls. The girls ran toward the door. Brown stood still blocking Booth's aim of the girls.

Booth yelled, "No!" and the girls froze. He motioned them to return to their seats.

Booth remained for a few minutes forcing Brown to ignore several incoming alarms from that area which the fire was growing. They stood without speaking. Schaefer groaned on the floor.

The girls couldn't help but somehow admire the dashing man with the gun. Booth's charisma was almost palpable to them. They suppressed smiles whenever he glanced their way.

Pulling out his pocket watch, he nodded in self-satisfaction.

"Thank you very much for that very enlightening tour. I have spent enough time enjoying your companionship in this lovely establishment. I believe I have caused enough of a sufficient delay in your fire department's response. Now I bid you ladies, adieu. Parting is such sweet sorrow," Booth said as he tipped his derby with a flourish. He waved the gun and exited.

Maggie let out a little giggle and Brown glared at her.

Brown helped Schaefer to his feet.

"Matthias, we need to alert the police," he said.

Schaefer let out a guffaw.

"Don't be ridiculous. Who'd believe that a mad fool held a gun on us to purposely misdirect the fire teams?"

"It's the truth!" Brown insisted.

"It's a damn fool thing, too. Listen to yourself. It sounds like you're making an excuse," Schaefer spit out a tiny bit of blood. "We'll just say we made a mistake. That everyone will believe. That they'll forgive. Tell them the truth that some madman held a gun on us? They'll think we're making up excuses. That they won't forgive."

Brown had to admit to the logic of it. Also he deferred to Schaefer's years of experience in dealing with the politics in the Chicago Fire Department. Brown hoped for a long career.

They shook on it.

CHAPTER 11

Avers opened his eyes. He was flat on his back and his shoulder ached. His eyes cleared as saw Bruno Goll kneeling over him waving a small bottle of smelling salts under his nose.

Avers sat up almost knocking Goll over. Goll had a large bump on his forehead. His vest was unbuttoned and his shirt ripped at the shoulder. A bandage taped underneath. His blazer was rolled up and under his head. His collar unbuttoned.

"Are you okay?"

"Ja, I'm fine, Just a little bump. But you. He shot you in the shoulder. Bullet went through. Broke a bottle. I bandaged you up." Goll said. "You lucky he didn't kill you."

"Luck had nothing to do with it. Booth is a horrible shot. When he shot President Lincoln, he used a derringer and had to hold it directly behind the President's ear. My Colt pistol is larger, heavier and I was a good five feet away. I'm surprised he hit me at all."

"Shot President Lincoln? But isn't that man?" Goll looked at Avers like he was a crazy man. He wondered if he did the right thing by mending this deluded fool's gunshot wound.

Avers was well-acquainted with the look on Goll's face. He realized that Goll was questioning his sanity as so many others did in the past.

"How long was I out?" Avers asked in an effort to change the subject.

"About thirty minutes, I guess."

"And where's Booth?"

"Who?" Goll leaned further away from the wounded man.

"The man with the gun!" Avers said exasperated.

"He asked about the Courthouse. The dummkopf wanted to know where was the Courthouse."

"That doesn't make sense. St. Paul's is his second target?"

"Ach, that church is not far from here. But the Courthouse?"

Avers rolled over and got up off the floor. He picked up his blazer, shook it out, and slipped it on. He thanked Goll and ran out the back door.

Goll shook his head. He could make no sense of the actions of these Americans ever since he came to this country.

Avers stood in the doorway. He saw his horse was gone. He expected Booth and his horse not to be there. But he didn't expect Booth would steal his horse as well.

Goll ran out after Avers. He held out a small tube.

"This is pain killer. It numbed your shoulder. It should be good for a few hours until you get to doctor," Goll said handing Avers the tube.

Avers slid the tube into his blazer pocket and thanked Goll again.

With no other option and not being familiar with the area, Avers ran back to the burning barn for help. He remembered that a horse was tied to a post by the O'Leary barn.

CHAPTER 12

Avers sprinted out of the drugstore and up Canal Street. He was drawn to the ghostly yellowish-orange glow in the northwestern sky like a moth to a flame.

In thirty minutes, the small barn fire expanded to consume the entire block along De Koven Street to Canal. It spread north and east and fast. Fire fighters ripped up the wooden sidewalk along De Koven. The combustible planks were removed, preventing not just the spread of the flames, but also served as fuel for the steamers' boilers. Hoses sprayed water up into the air to soak roofs and fences. Sullivan and Regan now aided in the fire fight by tossing buckets of water onto the barn.

Avers roamed along the south road side of De Koven recognizing the same fire fighters from the night before as they faced yet another city blockwide blaze. The same men, tired and battle worn, used the same equipment, overworked and battered from the previous night.

America and Little Giant were the first engines to reach De Koven. America was merely a hose cart with limited water-throwing capability. Little Giant arrived soon afterward. Showing dents and scorch marks from the fire fight the night before, Little Giant once again forced water through its fatigued hoses. The attempts to quell the flames appeared trivial. The increasing southern wind lifted sparks and embers east to more sheds, more houses, and more fences, all dry kindling. Leaves and dry grass pushed flames low to trap them in the unoccupied oxygen-rich spaces underneath the sidewalks.

The trees along De Koven Street helped transport fire down the block. Even ones at a distance from another were assisted by the wind to stretch their branches and pass the torch down the line.

As the block was destroyed, seven additional fire brigades entered the fray. Additional hose carts arrived. More companies assisted in the futile attempt to control the chaos.

Avers recognized Chief Fire Marshall Williams as he arrived with the seven fire engines.

Seeing pipemen working the hose cart, America, Williams encouraged them. "Hold on to her, boys. She's gaining on us!"

A foreman of another company hustled over to Williams. "Fire Engine No. 5 arrived but just broke down, sir," he reported.

"Douse the flames. Pour everything we have on it," Williams commanded.

"Marshall, I don't believe we can stand it here!" yelled one of the men.

"The smoke, the heat, is engulfing them, sir," said a nearby foreman.

"Stand it as long as you can," urged Williams the men.

"The water's evaporating as soon as it hits the houses," yelled another fireman.

Williams turned to the foreman.

"Turn in a second alarm," he ordered, "This is going to spread."

Avers overheard the order and told the foreman about the alarm at Goll's store.

"How long has this fire been burning?" asked Williams.

"About an hour," Avers answered.

"The fire's pushing us back," shoured Charles Anderson, another fire-fighter.

"Details, man, details," demanded Williams.

"Charley McConners used a door as a fire shield. It burst into flame in no time, sir. A steam pump stopped working. Four hoses burst." Anderson added.

"Use blankets to mend them" Williams responded.

"Steamers are losing steam, sir. Hoses springing leaks," he continued.

Williams grimaced at the news.

"Without pressure, the men have got to get closer to the fire," Anderson declared.

"I'm well aware of what that means. Damn," swore Williams.

"All due respect, sir, you can see my clothes are smoldering. The heat twisted my hat, sir," Anderson said with a tinge of exasperation.

"Re-position those engines," ordered Williams, pointing to the carts along De Koven. "Come out as fast as possible. Wet the other side of the street or it'll burn."

Williams helped with the hoses. He looked up helplessly at the firefly-like floating embers overhead.

"It's too late. Everything's going wrong," sighed Anderson.

Avers realized the fire fighter was right. But it wasn't due to anything wrong on Williams' part.

The dry season combined with an increasing wind worked against the efforts. Less than an inch of rain fell in almost a month. Wood, being the primary building material, acted as kindling dried by hot winds. Sidewalks and buildings, raised off the ground due to Chicago's natural swampy surroundings, allowed fire to spread underneath like a draft.

Both man and machine were pushed to their limits. The first week of October counted more than fifteen fires. All two hundred and eight fire department men were on call twenty-four hours a day. Most of those men suffered from inflamed eyes, smoke poisoning, and lack of sleep. Additionally, two engines were unavailable, both in need of repair.

Booth's misdirection at the Courthouse complicated firefighting efforts as well.

Avers resisted the urge to assist in the fire fighting. He needed to catch

Booth before he set St. Paul's on fire.

Avers was stymied. The reason he returned to this site was inconsequential now. The horse and indeed all the animals in the barn were either dead or removed to safety. Any other available horses were hauling wagons used in battling the blaze.

Avers looked around for any available method of transportation.

He watched people leaving their homes whether it was willingly or dragged out by family members or fire men.

Streets gave the illusion of breathing from being lit up by flickering flames.

Scalding heat outraced before tongues of flames.

Smoke and charred wood reeked throughout the neighborhood.

Then he pinpointed a familiar face.

CHAPTER 13

Avers recognized Richard F. Cromie in his customary dark suit and tie as he set up his camera. Once again Cromie used the large trunk as an improvised tripod base for his camera. Inside the trunk was a fresh supply of glass photographic plates.

Cromie focused his camera for a spectacular scene of the disaster. He imagined it as front page material.

"Where's St. Paul?" blurted out Avers as he approached Cromie.

Cromie quickly snapped a photograph of the firemen tearing up planks of the wooden sidewalk in front of the O'Leary home. He framed the action with houses engulfed in flames in the background and people gathering buckets of water at the side. He excluded the burning trees in front.

"Where's St. Paul's Church?" Avers said again tugging at Cromie's shoulder.

"What are you talking about? Here's the story!" Cromie pulled away from Avers.

"No, it's not. This is where it started! I know who started it. I saw him do it. I know where he's headed next!" Avers shouted.

Cromie looked at him and saw the earnest face. He removed the plate and wrapped it up in a velvet cloth. He grabbed another plate and inserted it into the camera.

"So this was planned?" Cromie said as he lined up a shot of policemen tearing down a wooden shed before it caught fire.

"You said you knew every inch of Chicago. Where's St. Paul's Catholic Church?" Avers pleaded.

"St. Paul's Catholic Church is on Mather Street just east of Clinton. About four blocks north of here," Cromie said as he placed the protected plate inside the trunk.

Cromie noticed how the flames began to take the vague shape of a tornado. The searing heat was uneven as it pressed against him and Avers. Sparks flew like red and yellow rain drops getting ever closer to his camera, his livelihood.

"Let's go," Avers urged. He grabbed the trunk and started dragging it north.

Cromie shrugged. "It's getting a little crowded there anyway. Chamberlain from the Evening Post and another Tribune reporter, Gus, just showed up."

Cromie tagged along partly to remove himself from the danger but mostly because that trunk contained his glass photographic plates and other supplies. He tightly gripped his camera close to his chest.

"Follow me and be careful with that," Cromie grumbled as he jogged in front of Avers.

Yanking the trunk onto his uninjured shoulder, Avers followed Cromie north on Clinton with the fire jumping behind them trying to keep up.

"So who's the arsonist? One of the men who called the alarm?" asked Cromie.

"No, they're merely dupes. Used by a despicable man. The personification of evil," Avers huffed as he lugged the truck in his shoulder and taking large steps. The gunshot wound still numb from Goll's ointment.

"Personification of evil, I like that. Mind of I use it in the article?"

Avers nodded and continued his dogged pursuit.

"What would make a man the personification of evil and not a mere arsonist?" Cromie pressed.

"He plans to set fire to a Catholic church, if he hasn't done so already! Because of his hatred of Catholicism. Just like his hatred of immigrants induced him to set a fire in the Irish ghetto. He needs to be tried. And hung!"

"What's his name?"

Avers stopped and stared solemnly at Cromie. He knew what to expect. He experienced the same reaction from people for more than six years.

"John Wilkes Booth."

Cromie stopped. He gazed at Avers with sympathy.

" SO WHO'S THE ARSONIST ? "

Avers set the trunk down. They were just two blocks away from St. Paul's.

"What's your racket?" Cromie asked skeptically.

"I know. I know," Avers said dryly. "I've heard it before. I had to resign my commission in the Army because of it. I can explain if we keep walking."

Avers lugged the trunk on his back again and continued north toward St. Paul's Church past Cromie.

Whether he felt sorry for the man or whether he had witnessed enough occasional outlandish situations as a journalist or whether he was amused at the concept, Cromie fell in step. He jogged next to Avers, partially because his photography supplies were in that trunk, partially because the heat from the fire approached, and partially because he wanted proof if it truly existed.

"I was part of the 16th New York Cavalry Regiment sent to capture Booth in Virginia. And a man was shot and killed in that burning barn. But the description of Booth matched many men at that time. Tall, dark hair, mustached. My suspicions were aroused when the body was abruptly dragged to a docked ship, instead of a hospital on land."

"That's right. I remember it was the Montark," Cromie added.

"Yes, the autopsy was performed on the ship by the Surgeon General. A couple people on the ship identified it as Booth but I know they never met Booth. They said as much to me. Booth's description that was provided to the members of the regiment included a short left leg, a scar on his neck, a distorted right thumb, and a hand drawn tattoo of J.W.B. on his left hand."

"Didn't any one check for that?"

"Not at first. A photographer from Washington was called in to identify the body. In fact, he took a photograph and a government detective took the plate and the print directly to the War Department. I know because I was ordered to be the military escort for Wardell, the detective, back to Washington."

"So, didn't that verify?"

"The plate and print vanished after the detective handed them to some government official in the State Department. I returned to my regiment in New York. By then, I had more information about Booth. I familiarized myself with several more photographs of him."

Cromie raised his eyebrow. Now Avers knew Cromie was interested.

"I performed my duties but on my time off, I delved further. I learned that no stage acquaintances, personal friends, relations, or co-conspirators were questioned in regards to identification. All of which were readily available. Including his mother and his brother, the famous Edwin Booth."

"This is very interesting, but…"

"I saw him. A few months after he 'died,' I saw him in New York. Edwin Booth agreed to meet with me. Talk with me. I saw his brother in a bar near a theater where Edwin was performing. I knew it was him. I reported it to my superior, Lt. Col. Campbell, but was told I was wrong. My duties were increased and my subsequent leaves were cancelled."

"Still?"

"I resigned my commission and began to track him. He…"

Cromie interrupted. "That would've been more than six years ago."

"Yes. I know."

"You've been tracking him for six years. In all that time didn't you gather any real proof?"

"That's where you come in. You have a camera. He's in Chicago now. I can take you to him. He'll be at the church soon if he's not there already. You can decide if I'm wrong."

"What?"

"You can see him face-to-face."

"I've seen all the same pictures that everyone else has. I doubt I can recall what he looks like."

"Once you see him, you'll remember."

Cromie was persuaded but still not completely convinced.

What a sensational story it would be if it were true, he thought. Still, catching an arsonist in the act of setting fire to church especially with a photograph would make headlines even with a month of fires reported daily.

Cromie and Avers came to an intersection. Cromie jerked his thumb to the right and Avers lugged the trunk east on Mather. They silently approached a stately structure of spiritual sanctuary and renewal on the south side of Mather. A round stain glass window of what Avers assumed was St. Paul welcoming parishioners glowed above the entrance.

A light source partially illuminated behind St. Paul's feet.

The area leading to the church was populated with wooden homes, fences, and sidewalks, all dried out from the unseasonably warm weather and naturally receptive to combustion.

Flames leapt from roof to roof a block behind them.

"The fire line encroached closer and closer," Cromie thought would be a great opening line of the article.

But the smell of burning wood and brush with grayish-green smoke preceded the fire as a warning. The wind forced the odor and fumes toward the photographer and the former soldier.

With the fire safely behind them, Avers set the trunk down and scanned the quietude around the church. As if to tempt a fiery fate, the church was adjacent to factories, woodworking shops, and a shingle mill.

It was reminiscent of the previous night. The thought was shared by both of them but not to be spoken out loud as if to jinx the situation.

Cinders floated harmlessly from behind and against the august structure. Eerie malevolent shadows flickered around and in front of the gothic structure.

"Set up here," Avers commanded as he plunked down the trunk in front of the steps of St. Paul's.

Avers heard a horse snort. Booth's horse was tied to the post on the side of the church. He let Cromie go about his business.

Walking closer to the gelding, the horse snorted again and held its head high. Avers knew a horse's snort indicated it perceived a threat. He noticed the tall church entry door was open. Avers untied the horse and shooed it away. The horse was very receptive to getting away as far as possible from the oncoming fire.

Silently, Avers sprinted up the cement steps and snuck inside. The only light he saw was from votive candles flickering along the sides. He crouched in the foyer waiting for any sign of movement. His patience paid off as he watched a rack of candles rise and crash against a wooden pew. The wax and oils from the candles spattered across the pew and accelerated the flames.

Booth burst out laughing.

"Let that Roman tyrant scrape money from his immigrant scum to refurnish this shrine to its foreign cult!"

"Have you no respect? I'll see you hang for your crimes."

"This faith, this cult takes its orders not from an American preacher, but a foreigner! Immigrant scum shove it in the face of good Americans! Oh, to set fire to this church for being Catholic and catering to Irish immigrants and decontaminate it for the sake of our own beloved country."

Avers found Booth's fondness for posturing dramatic speeches tiresome. In an effort to shut him up, he rushed Booth. Automatically, Booth raised the Colt.

Booth pulled the trigger as Avers dove between the black walnut pews. Wood splintered near Avers. Booth charged toward Avers as flames escalated from one wooden pew to another. Avers wiggled underneath to escape the flames and dodged Booth by rolling through the foyer and out the door.

"Here he comes," shouted Avers as he somersaulted out the door.

Cromie snapped a photograph as Booth and flames followed Avers out the door. The flash attracted Booth's attention. Instinctively, Booth smiled and bowed. A gust of wind blew the derby off his head.

"You got a photograph of him?" Avers said standing up at the foot of the steps.

"I think so," Cromie said from the street.

Booth capered down the church steps and moved over where his horse should have been. Realizing it was gone; he pointed his gun toward Cromie but pulled back.

"I do hope you got my good side, sir," he smirked as he faced Cromie.

Cromie squinted trying to distinguish the features of the man's face between the interior fire and dim street lamp. The contrast in illumination caused mocking shadows across his face. Booth stepped onto the sidewalk between Avers and Cromie to afford Cromie a better view.

"He's a journalist. A newspaperman. Taking a photograph for the newspaper," Avers said. Mentally he was estimating if Booth was close enough to throw the knife at him. If he missed, he might strike Cromie.

"I am well aware what a newspaperman is, ass. I've suffered enough at the hands of so-called theater critics," Booth said with a gleam in his eye.

A noisy crowd formed across the street from the church. Most had staggered across the bridge from saloons in Conley's Patch to get a better view of the South Side fire. Booth hesitated as this new audience swelled.

Someone in the forming crowd of spectators shouted and pointed up.

A firebrand, a flaming two-by-four, drifted from some random lumberyard across Clinton Street above their heads. The wind gently guided it to the top of the church. Another piece hovered nearby and dipped straight into the wooden steeple. Like a pre-heated oven, the heat from below allowed the flames to mushroom promptly up through the church. Within what seemed like moments the entire church was ravaged. The stained glass image of St. Paul shattered outward from the intensity of the heat.

The falling glass showered Avers, Cromie, and Booth.

An elderly woman with an Irish brogue standing in the rear of the crowd asked what was on fire. A tall man in front yelled back that it was St. Paul's Church.

The Irishwoman calmly responded, "Oh. God will put it out." She wandered back to her home.

Booth stifled another laugh. Avers stepped forward with the knife now in his hand. Booth leveled the Colt at him.

Captivated, the crowd stared upward as more flaming pieces of wood and cinders landed gently on the church. Each piece found a resting place on the church roof. Instead of dying out, each flame was welcomed and prospered.

Cromie wandered closer to get a better view of the man. His jaw dropped in recognition.

"Dear God in Heaven," Cromie exclaimed as he got a clear view of Booth's face.

Cromie's clear recognition made Booth beam with joy.

Booth saw him and bowed his head in acknowledgement.

"I must be off. I do hope we meet again."

Avers took another step toward Booth.

Booth aimed the long-barreled revolver toward the crowd. "I'm quite certain that I can shoot someone fatally in the group."

Avers and Cromie froze.

Four blocks to the south of this drama, firemen were still attacking various flames as if it was a game of hide and seek. One flame would be extinguished and another one would pop up nearby. Disregarding the human effort below, winds snatched pieces of burning lumber out of reach and sent them north and east.

The fire succeeded in proliferating to the lumberyards and mills around St. Paul's. The entire neighborhood became an inferno. Gawkers were milling waiting for something new to happen.

Not unexpectedly, the church's roof caved. As if in response, a hook-and-ladder team arrived on the scene to extinguish this new blaze. The spectators cheered as if it was a sporting event. To make way for the fire engines, the crowd shifted to northwest corner under a sign that read "Garden City."

Fire men rushed in to rescue holy relics. Long planks were laid down on the steps to allow safer access inside and out. Two hoses sprayed water on the church's sides. The ladder on the hook-and-ladder broke. Another steamer pulled up to the side of the church on Clinton.

In the organized confusion, Booth escaped.

Avers pushed away from the crowd to locate Booth. Cromie gripped Avers' arm to stop him.

Cromie pointed west where flames formed into a whirlwind shape. "A fire devil!"

CHAPTER 14

A fire devil is, in essence, what fire fighters call a flame-and-ash torna-do caused by the intense heat of a fire combining with cooler strong winds. Heat above the fire siphons the cooler air below into a turbulent rotation. The convection of air and flame forms a whirlwind of death and destruction. It can grow to be ten-stories high.

One, the size of the church, was bearing down on Avers and Cromie.

They and the crowd on the corner started to back away from the fire devil. Blocked by the firefighting efforts to east, the mob considered avenues of retreat. First they swung en masse to the south but the fire spread its arms into the neighborhood of wooden structures. The people meandered north and the southern wind encouraged flames in the direction. Finally random men, women, and children screamed and cowered instead of escaping in any direction. Sparks charred any exposed clothing including Cromie's suit jacket.

Avers looked up and, by the light of the church fire, was able to read the entire sign that people cowered under. Large, bold letters was plainly written "Garden City," and in smaller letters was "Match Factory." As the fire devil rose overhead, he separated from the crowd. His grip tightened on the trunk's strap. He headed north as the wind now blew east.

"Booth, be damned," he thought as he marched north along Clinton Street with Cromie in tow.

People seeing fire at the west, south, and east intuitively followed Avers and Cromie who marched decisively north.

"I can't believe it's him," Cromie whispered over and over.

The wind shifted again. One, two, three blocks later, the fire devil continued to hunt them northward. Scared men clung to their crying wives and whimpering children. All mindlessly followed in dire hopes that the two men knew where they were going.

Pushed by the building southern winds, the fire devil bore down on them. Flames leapt from shop to factory to shack. Tongues of the fire washed the sidewalk and licked alongside the refugees.

Blistering heat pressed Avers forward north until finally he led the frightened group to a safe haven. They filed into the Red Flash district past Van Buren Street between Clinton and Canal Streets.

Cromie loosened and removed his necktie letting it flutter away in the wind. His singed suit jacket tried to take wing in pursuit of its partner. He let the cool air embrace him.

The conflagration from the night before provided shelter from the new holocaust.

The fire devil halted because of the natural firebreak. There was nothing for the fire to consume. The previous night's wildfire gorged itself and left nothing for the tonight's fire devil to feast on. Unable to continue its feeding, it dissipated.

The former gawkers continued to walk north on Clinton into cooler temperatures. Wore out from the fear, they sat in the rubble and ashes to gather their strength and collect their thoughts. Blustery, the night air cooled their bodies.

Avers and Cromie pressed on as if the wind guided them.

"Where would he have gone next?" asked Avers.

"Definitely away from the fire," reasoned Cromie.

"But where? Are we near anything combustible?"

"The whole damn city is combustible!" Cromie shot back.

Avers stopped to focus his thoughts. He looked back at the group in the remnants of shops and homes. He was saddened at how they were so willing to witness tragedy and so ill prepared to face it.

"Where's the nearest saloon?" Avers asked.

"You want to drink at a time like this?" Cromie said baffled.

"No. Well, yes I could use a drink. That fire devil made me a little parched. But I've always found saloons to be an excellent source of information," Avers answered.

Then the answer dawned on Avers.

"The saloon where the bartender handed out free drinks and kept it from burning down!"

"Daniel Quirk's place?"

"Yes, the font of all wisdom," Avers joked.

Avers reacted without hesitation. Blindly he started walking east toward the Van Buren Street Bridge.

Cromie groaned as he knew he had to follow Avers. The obsessed fool had his photographic equipment and plates on his back. The newspaper man in Cromie realized this was an important news story was in the making. Oddly, a protective fondness swelled in Cromie like an experienced guide develops for hapless wanderer entrusted in his care.

Cromie jogged over to Avers.

"Wrong way, Phil."

Cromie headed north. He stopped, looked at Avers, and jerked his head. Avers followed silently.

Located a block and a half away, Quirk's saloon did a brisk business in spite of the desolation across the street.

Avers and Cromie entered the saloon. None of the patrons took notice. They sidled up to the long wooden bar with the trunk and still the drinking continued unabated.

Avers ordered a beer and Cromie requested a whiskey. Then they leaned back and listened.

Naturally, bits of conversation rambled on about personal exploits of the night before.

Sensing the congenial atmosphere, Avers joined in.

"There's another one burning tonight," he injected after a slovenly-dressed gentleman finished his tale about rescuing a half-naked woman who thanked him carnally.

That statement caused everyone in the saloon to stop talking and take notice of the newcomers and their rather large suitcase.

"Whach yer mean?"

"If you look out the door, the entire South Side is on fire," Avers said as he finished his mug.

The patrons focused their attention to a man with a long brown beard sitting nearest the door.

The man took a gulp of his drink and reluctantly staggered over to the door. He opened the door and stuck his head out. His shaggy head retreated and he resumed his seat without saying a word. After taking a deep breath, he nodded.

Livelier discussions now erupted and Avers and Cromie just absorbed it and waited.

"The South Side Gas Works is just across the river over there. Like that dude said that could be next, you know."

Once they heard that they knew. Leaving payment for their drinks, Avers and Cromie proceeded out the door. Again no one in the saloon took notice.

Gathering that piece of vital information took all of two minutes.

Avers hesitated but Cromie knew where to go.

Cromie crossed over the sidewalk and east from the corner. Avers trailed behind.

"You're pretty good at that," Cromie said. "But, of course, that's only one way to cultivate a source."

"Been doing it for six years. I know his habits. He likes saloons and an audience. Figured he'd stop in one and say something to someone," Avers acknowledged.

"The Gas Works is just over the bridge," Cromie signaled the direction with a nod of his head.

The night was too dark to see any of the previous night's charred marks on the trestles or girders. But they could see the fires burning southwest of them. A gale pushed them and burning cinders across the river.

Windblown glowing embers flowed in that direction.

Fiery residue from the fire devil drifted across the south branch of the Chicago River to Parmelee Omnibus and Stage Co. at Franklin and Jackson Streets. The roof of the three-story building was soon ablaze. It was scheduled to open in three days.

"Six years? In all that time, haven't you wanted to just give up?"

"Of course, I have," Avers shrugged. "I've tried walking away from this several times. I was in the Army for almost a year after Booth assassinated President Lincoln. Then I tracked him down South, then to the Hawaiian islands. I worked a sugar plantation in Honolulu for almost a year there." A wistful smile crossed Avers' face.

"Then Booth up and leaves for Europe. I was a bartender in Germany for a few months, I saw him during Oktoberfest. Then the hunt was on again. Something always drew me back to him. I tried to walk away. Tried to forget but I couldn't. I'd hear something. I'd see something. He'd do something to attract my attention. He'd hurt somebody. Sometimes it feels like I can only make a difference by stopping someone from being hurt by his evil. He seems impervious."

"That's the most I've ever heard you utter at one time," Cromie joked.

Within one block of crossing the bridge, Cromie turned north on Market Street with Avers and trunk at his side. At the end of the block, Avers saw a sign "Chicago Gas Light and Coke Co." painted on a two-story brick building on the south side of the street. "Are we near the South Side Gas Works?"

"That's it over there," Cromie said pointing to the building. "Everyone just calls it The South Side Gas Works."

The South Side Gas Works provided illuminating gas to the south side around the Chicago River for the last 21 years. Along the west side of the street were brick buildings that housed furnaces, purifying apparatus, station meters, and gas regulators. In its yard next to the main station plant were tool, coal, and wagon sheds with a large barn—all wooden structures with piles of coal and barrels of tar stacked next to them.

Avers rested the trunk in the dirt street beside the Gas Works. Since no fence encircled the yard, he entered unencumbered. Once again he checked for any sign of movement in the dim gas lights and shadows. He sensed Booth was nearby.

Cromie walked closer to the river to set up his camera to photograph the blaze behind them.

At the west end of the yard, Booth rummaged in a coal shed. He couldn't locate any kerosene, lamps, gasoline, or candles that would ignite quickly. Shrugging his shoulders, he felt his search was futile.

As if in response to his frustration, a burning shingle dropped out of the sky in front of the shed.

Booth's eyes lit up.

"God's will" is all he whispered as he stooped to pick it up.

Flinging it by its unlit corner, Booth tossed the burning shingle into the air. It sailed into an adjacent open coal tar tank near the main building.

Booth ducked out of the coal shed and ran far from the volatile gas lines. He pinched his nose to stop smelling the stink of the coal tar.

"Booth!" Avers screamed from the east end of the yard.

Booth halted as if he was yanked by a rope. With his right hand, he unpinched his nose and pulled the Colt from his belt. He spun around slowly on his heel. His face was a grimace. Then it slowly twisted into a smile.

He took a deep bow as if to say 'how delightful to see you.'

Avers broke into a sprint with his hand forming claws. His singular focus was wrapping his hands around Booth's throat. His feet stretched into yard-length strides.

Booth whipped out the Colt again and aimed at Avers. Avers did not slow his pace. Then Booth shifted his aim toward Cromie in the street.

Cromie was oblivious. He was fixated in trying to get the flames on the river in the correct frame for his camera. Years of lumberyards and meat-packing plants dumping slimy waste into the river created pockets of flammable grease and oil. Even a block away, islands of flames visibly dotted the riverscape among cargo ships and tug boats. A magnificent perspective thought Cromie that would make even an editor like Horace White stand up and take notice.

Avers froze in place. He knew Booth wasn't a skilled shooter but he might squeeze off a lucky shot. A protective fondness swelled in Avers like an experienced guide develops for a hapless wanderer entrusted to his care.

In that moment of hesitation, oily flames burst over the tank onto the shed and up the building. It rapidly torched the wooden window frames. Even shattering of glass didn't compel Cromie to lose focus.

Booth laughed waiting for the gas pipes and storage tanks to explode. Neither of them moved.

After several seconds, Booth frowned. "Why isn't this blowing up?"

CHAPTER 15

Thomas Ockerby never achieved fame. He earned his promotions because he was diligent at his job and had that rare quality—common sense. Ockerby was the night superintendent of the Chicago Gas Light and Coke Co. and he was worthy of the position.

Seeing something glowing in the night sky float across the river and the Parmelee Omnibus and Stage Co. catch fire, he wasted no time in re-routing the reserve gas out of the division reservoirs to the tanks on the new North side station. By working the valves, he directed explosive gas out of the oncoming fire's path. This prevented unnecessary catastrophe.

By the time Booth set the coal shed on fire, Ockerby averted an explosion by merely acting responsibly. He then focused on the safety of buildings by leading his crew into the yard.

Avers' eyes re-adjusted between the eerie darkness and flickering light.

Ockerby ran out of the building past Avers. Immediately, the rest of the gas house gang streamed out also ignoring the former soldier.

Ockerby poised in the middle of the yard issued orders.

"Hose down that shed. Fill up those buckets with water. Get them up to the roof. You, men on the roof. Stamp out those fires. Go to the main barn and, for God's sake, unhitch the horses."

Noticing Booth and Avers, Ockerby pointed at them.

"Get those men out of here!"

Next Ockerby helped connect a hose to a nearby fire hydrant. After it was connected, he ran to the saloon across Market Street to warn of the oncoming fire.

"Go home," he shouted. "Don't let your roof catch on fire."

Returning to the gas works yard, Ockerby was climbed up the retort house for a better view of the yard.

"Hose down that tank!" he waved to two men holding the hose. The tank contained roofing tar, a by-product of the gas works. Extremely flammable roofing tar.

"I said get those men out of here," glaring at Avers and Booth.

Booth exited the yard before anyone could grab him.

A brawny man gripped Avers by the arm.

Flames erupted by a storage tank taller than any man in the yard.

"Get more buckets over there by that gasholder," Ockerby commanded. "Go to the shed. See if there are horses there. Get them out if there are!"

He pointed to a small barn where sizzling could be heard. No flames could be seen from ground level. The tar barrels behind it were on fire.

He slid down from the retort house and hurried over to the shed. Avers and the man joined him.

Yanking the doors wide open, they expelled a collective sigh of relief. No horses or any other animals were inside.

"It's the head superintendent's company buggy," Ockerby seizing the yoke. The brawny man lifted the other side of the yoke and helped him wheel it out.

Avers sidestepped the buggy and ducked in the shed. The ceiling was aflame now and lit up the inside of the shed. Avers saw the only other object in the shed—a wooden wheelbarrow filled with reins, straps, buckles, and hitches.

By the time, Ockerby and the man returned to salvage the buggy equipment, fire made the entire shed inaccessible.

"Where's the wheelbarrow?" asked Ockerby seeing reins, straps, buckles, and hitches spilled on the shed floor.

A young man, newly hired, ran up to Ockerby.

"There's a fire engine down the block."

Ocklerby was out of the yard and down Franklin Street in record time. Looking for a fireman issuing orders to other firemen, he identified the foreman. He approached the engine foreman.

"The Gas Works needs to be hosed down," Ockerby said.

"I'll not send my men there," the foreman replied.

"It's perfectly safe. I'll go down there with you."

"I do not take any man's soul in my hand. You can take the lead in there if you want to."

The engine foreman turned his attention elsewhere.

Ockerby seizing the nearest fire hose, lugged it through the alley and into back of the yard. Unprepared for the power, the hose forced him back as the water gushed out of it.

His men tried to steady Ockerby but wound up getting hosed down by him instead. Water sprayed uncontrollably. Water hit the main plant. Then it landed on the roofs of the sheds and on top of the tanks. Then it poured into the street.

Cromie, satisfied with the photographs of the river and Gas Works, packed up his equipment. He locked the trunk and gripped its strap handle. He dragged the trunk east on Monroe Street. The trunk dug a wide groove in the dirt in the street. He wanted to get it out of the way of the wildly spraying water.

Ockerby and his men quickly tamed the hose and focused their firefighting efforts.

Within minutes, firemen shut off the water and reclaimed the hose.

Although no gas explosion occurred, flames overtook the Gas Works' station, sheds, barrels, and coal piles despite Ockerby's efforts.

As the offices and plant in the Gas Works went up in flames, the roof crashed in. All pipes and valves were crushed. Without the Gas Works in operation, street lights dimmed. Lights in homes and shops and saloons blinked. The streets of Chicago were plunging into darkness. The remaining gas supply began to leak out of the pipeline. Within an hour, the only illumination would be from the devastating fires

Cromie stopped moving. He heard rumbling and thumping on the sidewalk to the north of him. He was unable to identify the source of the commotion. The flickering lights distorted moving figures.

Out of the shadows emerged Avers. Without asking Cromie, Avers hoisted the trunk into the wheelbarrow. Gripping the arms of the wheelbarrow, Avers pushed the wheelbarrow east.

"Let's get out of here," Avers said.

Avers knew Booth was headed into Conley's Patch and he was none too happy about it.

Unable to do more, the gas house workers escaped the fire by heading north to the Madison Street Bridge.

The last thing Avers and Cromie heard was Ockerby shouting.

"What the hell happened to that damn wheelbarrow?"

" LET'S GET OUT OF HERE. "

CHAPTER 16

A vice-ridden slum, Conley's Patch, radiated over several blocks. Its wickedness and immorality oozed out from its center. Fire hopped from dirty, ramshackle shanty after dirty, ramshackle shanty that tightly packed its landscape. It was almost as if it was cleansing the hub of social outcasts and criminals of all sorts that inhabited this section mere blocks east of the river's south branch.

Its squat hovels, pawnshops, and saloons were already devoured by flames. Brothels, shacks, and outhouses lit up like torches on both sides of the street. The fire traveled from the top down from almost one hunderd feet in the air. Flames, not smoke, blotted out every cloud and star in the autumn night sky. The crackle and roar of the fire drowned out any sound of man. Heat acquired the consistency of molasses. The smell of human sweat competed with white-hot wood to sting the nose.

It was after midnight when Avers pushed the trunk-laden wheelbarrow into Conley's Patch. This was the fourth time Avers had invaded that disgusting piece of land. He silently vowed it was his last.

Avers should have looked like a ridiculous itinerant pushing a loaded wheelbarrow down the middle of the street chasing Booth. But he joined the horde of people already in the streets—a mob carrying packs on their backs, in wagons, and on carts.

Market Street felt uninhabited to Avers and Cromie in comparison to Adams Street. Trying to flee to safety, the dozens of inhabitants of Conley's Patch sought refuge on the west side of the Adams Street Bridge.

But now its trestles and guard rails were on fire. So the mass migration reversed itself through Conley's Patch which now closely resembled the pits of Hell.

The throng in the street shrieked and swallowed Booth in their midst.

Searching for Booth in the faces of the crowd, Avers and Cromie observed scared, confused, and determined expressions, mixed together. A barefoot little girl carried a box with four puppies in it. Two boys crying for their parents held candy tight in their grip. A grimy man protectively tucked window blinds under his arm. A resolute fat man wielded a length of stovepipe in front of him. A young scruffy-looking man carried his bearded grandfather on his back. Two men hauled a wooden Indian between them. A cigar dealer closely followed them with an armful of cigar boxes.

A Negro woman balanced a basket of clothes on her shoulder and another basket filled with a frying pan and muffin rings. When the clothes started burning, she dumped it in the street and left it behind.

A man single-handedly pulling a horse buggy ran over the basket. Inside the buggy, a woman wearing only a nightgown held whatever goods they could grab.

In escaping the fire, people dressed quickly and haphazardly. One young man wore a woman's dress over a long linen duster. Another man was dressing in an evening gown. Women in night gowns or men's trousers did not attract attention. Ripped button-down shirts were as common as scorched calico blouses. Hats, shawls, and head scarves were blown away in the wind and further kindled the surrounding flames.

Animals did not escape the wrath of the flames. Pets ran over fences or were trapped in homes. Wandering in the crowd, an elderly man mourned for his lost dog. Brown rats scurried across feet and were crushed under wheels. Pigeons flew into smoke and fire or were blown by the wind to their death. Bewildered pigs, goats and cows rambled through the streets alongside humans seeking safe shelter. A rooster dodged footsteps and wheels.

People continued to swarm out of their dwellings with whatever they could carry or put on anything with wheels. Rough women carried crying babies and bundles of clothes. Coarse men carried disheveled children and kegs of beer. Wagons, drays, and carts were filled with whatever could be collected in a moment's notice.

Some of the denizens of Conley's Patch looted saloons or stayed and drank for free. Brutish men carrying liquor bottles or a barrel were as common as scared women clutching their children or clothes. Those were the ones that escaped.

Avers tried to block out the desperate screams within the flaming shacks. His focus was Booth who reveled in this chaos. He set down the wheelbarrow to one side.

Avers could see abandoned elderly people inside burning shanties. Families were on the roofs of tenements with no way to descend. No trees grew in Conley's Patch.

Drunks lapped up whiskey from smashed barrels leaking into the gutters.

Avers froze. He felt smothered by the smoke and heat. Hot cinders stung his eyes. The stench of burnt wood and flesh overwhelmed his sense of smell. He could hear the fire breathe in the wind to expand its path. Screams from inside the buildings and out in the streets echoed in his ears. He kept his mouth shut so not to taste the ashen horror surrounding him.

Maybe the ill and infirmed needed to be weeded out, purged, and cauterized, from society just like Booth boasted.

A hard-faced man bumped into Avers knocking him out of his paralysis. The man spilled some alcohol out of the bottle he carried onto the head of a little girl. The man was more concerned with the booze he lost than the girl whose hair he set on fire.

Avers resisted the urge to flatten the self-absorbed drunk. He threw his blazer over the screaming girl. The flames on her head were snuffed out. Damage was done. The girl would be scarred for life. Maybe the hair would grow back, maybe it wouldn't. She pushed Avers away and scrambled into the crowd, still clenching his blazer to her head like a smoldering security blanket.

A small group kneeled in the street, blocking those trying to flee.

"It's the end of times!" a dark-haired woman past her prime screamed.

"Perdition is upon us!" another woman wept.

"Revelation is coming true!" a gray-haired man wailed with hands raised.

"The apocalypse . . ." choked a man.

They found it easier to give in than fight back.

Avers would fight back despite the ubiquitous flames.

Avers turned his attention to saving any one he could. In any small way, he'd make a difference by stopping someone from being hurt by Booth's despicable deeds. Even if it was just merely a few potential victims.

He broke down doors and pulled out anyone within reach. He placed the sick and elderly on carts and threatened whoever would try to stop him or charge him for the human cargo.

These may not be the most respectable members of the society, Avers thought, but they were people. And Avers would save some of them. Like he heard a fireman had done, he used a door as a shield to allow a family to escape from a roomful of flames.

Cromie caught up to Avers as another firebrand drifted into and set fire to a three-story framed tenement.

"What happened there?" Cromie pointed to Avers' bandaged shoulder. Without the blazer, the ripped sleeve and bandage were obvious.

"Booth's bad aim," Avers said and he was off again.

Avers pushed a man out of the burning tenement. The man tried to get around Avers saying he left something behind. Avers blocked him several times until the man relented.

Avers turned his attention to a screaming child across the street.

Cromie watched the man spin around and dash back to the tenement. He didn't step inside before the flaming building dropped on him. He didn't even have time to scream.

Cromie shut his eyes. This wasn't the first time he witnessed tragedy. He was numb to it after his years as a reporter. One could not last as a reporter if such human drama had an emotional impact.

Cromie, still just an observer, shook his head as Avers rescued helpless people from other burning tenements. He admired the tenacity even if the action proved futile.

One woman ran back inside her home after Avers pulled her out. He went back in after her. Back in the street, she wiggled from of him again. She returned inside her hovel. One more time Avers threw her over his shoulder. As he set her down, she took one step toward her home and it tumbled down in fires before she could get within ten feet of it. She shrugged and joined the exodus east.

The street was filled with Conley Patch natives who were either spectators or fleeing their homes with their meager possessions. And in the midst of it all, one man was heroically saving people from danger.

Besides burning buildings, falling fiery timbers and debris from the sky endangered the unprotected heads in the street. Avers and Cromie had to pat small flames out of their clothes from the falling embers.

Wagons and buggies weren't threats because the street was so tightly packed. But they were still obstacles to be dodged.

Resisting the crowds in the streets, Cromie set up his camera for photographs. He understood Avers' frustration. He knew they lost Booth again and he had to do something instead of just standing by.

The smoke cleared briefly enough for him to take a photograph of the tenement engulfed in flames. The fire burned brightly enough so no flash was needed.

Unknown to Cromie, he was next to the shack where Avers was beaten up earlier and killed a man about twelve hours earlier.

Looking among the crowd for the best angle of the chaos, Cromie heard shouting about the Ku Klux Klan. Cromie turned and saw Booth yelling.

Parodying the mob's fear, Booth ran around wildly and shouted, "I knew they would do it! I knew they would do it!" He stopped and stared at a terrified housewife with a child in her arms. He continued, "The Bloody Ku-Klux have done this, knowing us to have been extra loyal. They have burned our city and it is useless for us to attempt to escape, for they will burn us up too!"

With a twist of his head, Booth smiled broadly at Cromie. He was less than a block away.

"Phil, he's here. He's there!" Cromie shouted as he pointed to the crazy man now dancing in the street. He had an audience who enjoyed the bizarre spectacle but those seeking shelter ignored him.

Avers boosted an elderly woman into a horse-drawn wagon. Her clothes were burned, but she was not. Avers' hair and shirt were singed as well.

"Philip Avers! Booth is over there," Cromie shouted as he packed the trunk back in the wheelbarrow.

Hearing his name, Avers looked at the photographer. Then to the site Cromie was gesturing at, a laughing man trying to get their attention.

Avers smiled. He knew Booth had taken the bait.

Booth was cackling wildly as if the fire was under his complete control, doing his very bidding. He raised his arms as if to conjure more flames.

"It's God's Will!" he sang. No one in the streets cold argue with him.

Making sure the old woman was on her way to safety, Avers focused on Booth. He started toward him but the mob of dispossessed people did not allow easy access.

Booth strutted unmolested north on Wells Street from Avers and Cromie who was still lugging the wheelbarrow. He headed into the business district. It was still relatively clear of flames.

For the moment, the fire acted as if it was contented to gorge on Conley's Patch rather than feed on the business district. This allowed shop people more time to salvage goods by tossing them out windows and onto the wagons and drays stationed below.

The crush of people thinned out on Wells Street because it currently accommodated wheeled transports of every type. Storefronts and striped awnings lined the sidewalks.

Shop owners carried their individual goods out to any available wagon or cart. From upper level storerooms, clerks lowered baskets of various sundries by rope.

Cromie weaved the wheelbarrow between the half-laden wagons. The sporadic maze of ropes and baskets delayed Avers' pursuit of Booth. Booth danced between the baskets and ropes. Avers moved from the sidewalk into the street. It was easier to maneuver among drays and pushcarts.

Avers and Cromie eyed John Wilkes Booth stroll up to a female clerk standing under a darkly striped awning. He bowed and kissed the hand of the lovely woman dressed in a stain-covered frock. Whatever he said brought a smile to the distressed lady. He escorted her further down the sidewalk.

At the corner of Monroe and Wells, Avers and Cromie were gaining on Booth and his new-found friend. Seeing that his followers were closing in on him, Booth shoved the woman back toward them and shouted, "Get thee to a nunnery!"

They helped the stunned girl up quickly and pursued Booth.

As they got closer, some careless clerk tossed or dropped two bolts of fabric from a window above a tailor shop. Both bolts bounced off the awning below and struck the pursuers. The soft cloth was enough to stun them momentarily and afford Booth to widen the distance between them.

Aware of the hazard, Avers and Cromie successfully avoided more items flung from windows above shops.

CHAPTER 17

In the middle of a new swarm of people going east at Madison Street, Avers saw a burly-looking thug in a torn shirt and pants tugging at a cloth bundle in the hands of a petite blonde girl. The girl desperately held onto it.

Avers set down the wheelbarrow. Pushing people out of his way, he seized the smaller man under the arms and lifted him in the air. Startled, the man let go of the girl's bundle. Avers carried the man away from the girl as she pressed the bundle close to her chest. He chucked the bully to the other side of the street.

The bully knocked over a few men with who he collided when he landed. He got to his feet and made a fist. Taking in Avers' greater size, he thought better of it and ran away like a skittering rat.

The frightened girl ducked into an alley between two burning shops. She started crying and shouted. "Papa! Papa!" She spun around searching for any familiar face.

Avers kept an eye on her. She started coughing and rubbing her eyes. She staggered further down the street and into the alley. She wandered into the middle of some sort of construction. Piles of bricks alongside wooden beams, boards, barrels, boxes, and ladders surrounded her. Fire suddenly flared up beside her as smoke billowed around her.

Avers yelled for her to run.

She squinted quizzically at him and asked, "Was sagst du?"

"Wie heißt du?" Avers shouted.

"Claire" she answered.

Avers waved and pleaded, "Hergelaufen, Claire!"

Claire took a step toward him. A fiery wooden beam fell and blocked her path. She edged back to a cool spot near a pile of bricks and sat down. She covered her head with the bundle for protection and prayed.

"Von dort wegstehen," Avers shouted through the fire.

Her dress began to burn. Dropping her bundle, she used her hands to snuff out the flames. Panicking, Claire with part of her curls burned off started to climb a nearby pile of bricks. Her hands and feet blistered from the intense heat absorbed by the bricks.

Avers jumped through the thick smoke and flames. With one hand, he lifted Claire up by the back of her scorched dress. With the other, he picked up the wrapped bundle.

Avers protectively wrapped his arm around her and escaped.

Cromie, pushing the wheelbarrow, caught up to them.

"What language is that?"

"German," Avers grunted as he set Claire down and held her wrist. He was careful to avoid grasping her little burnt hand.

"You speak German?"

"I was in Germany. Tracked Booth there."

"How?"

"He was performing with a touring company. It traveled to England. That's where I met Mary and Tad."

Claire looked at the man who led her by the wrist. She couldn't understand the words he spoke. But the anger in the tone was clear to her.

"Tad Lincoln? That little brat!"

"Tad was maturing into a fine man. Had a bright future. Planning to go to Harvard like his brother. Definitely the makings of a talented politician. His father's name. His mother's guidance. Possible presidential material."

"Sorry about his death," Cromie said sensing Avers was defensive of Tad.

"Mary thought I was mad, of course. Like everyone else. But she and Tad consented to go to see him perform. Tad was very protective of his mother."

Cromie shrugged unbelieving.

"Mary was there when he was shot. Sitting next to Lincoln. She clearly saw Booth standing next to her. The woman has a wonderful mind, and the event etched in her memory."

Claire started to tug away from Avers. Her head twisted around trying to recognize a familiar face.

"When Booth came out on stage, Mary and Booth locked eyes. Mary, fine woman that she is, maintained her decorum. He ran off stage. But not before Tad memorized his face too. We lost track of him. We returned to America. Went our separate ways. After they encountered him a few months ago, here in Chicago, they contacted me. Mary hired me to track him down and capture him. Most of all, to prove that he killed Tad."

Claire was pulling away from Avers. He saw the unreasoning terror in her eyes. He realized she would break away at her first opportunity.

Not breaking their stride, Avers edged toward the side. A shop owner offering free hats to passers by attracted his attention. No one accepted these free offerings. Instead desperate men looted a dry goods store next door. Under the burning awning, a looter ran out laden with food. Avers dragged a scared Claire to the store. He grabbed apples and shoved them in her dress pockets. He put a wedge of cheese in her hand. She ran south as soon as he let go of her wrist

Avers grabbed a couple of apples for Cromie and himself. He offered a silent prayer for the petite girl.

Miraculously, twelve-year-old Claire Innes would return to her burnt out neighborhood and reunite safely with her parents and siblings by the next morning.

CHAPTER 18

Crunching on their apples, Avers and Cromie arrived at Washington Street and paused for any sign of Booth.

By now, the business district with its frame shops and shanties provided kindling to overheat stone banks and insurance companies. No matter how respectable the business—plumbing, carpenter, restaurant, bath house, clothing, or undertaking—fires assumed the appearance of Purgatory, absolving the district of the sin of greed.

Avers took noticed of how the telegraph poles in the business district replaced trees that were in the working class districts. Like the leaves, all the wires had been burned off. Unlike the trees in the south side, the poles were planted in an orderly fashion in the street next to the wooden side-walks. Also like the trees they easily lit up like massive torches.

"Hey, Philip! Wait!" Cromie shouted. "Philip. Stop!" He screamed as loud as possible. He kept on screaming until Avers finally heard him. He was unaware that he was still walking.

Cromie stopped and let go of the wheelbarrow. He pointed west. "We're near where I live." He headed west on Washington Street.

Avers hesitated. He looked at the diminishing figure of Booth strutting east and then over to Cromie running west.

Not moving, the wooden wheelbarrow and trunk started to smolder from sparks and intense heat coming from behind. Avers picked up the wheelbarrow and steered after Cromie. The western winds blew out any potential embers on the wheelbarrow and trunk.

Although just a block away from his residence, Cromie's path was impeded. Heat and wind and people shoved against Cromie who was going against the flow of traffic. Since the Washington Street Tunnel was impassable at this point, no other option to escape the impending calamity was available. In the middle of Washington Street, the tunnels occupied most of the roadway. Its three openings bellowed smoke. The entrance and exit for horsecarts and the pedestrian walkway offered no avenue to safety on the other side of the Chicago River.

At the southwest corner of Washington and Franklin, the year-old Nevada Hotel attracted orange, yellow, and red flames from its neighbors. Fire mixed those colors as it covered the rest of the neighborhood. Clouds of smoke swirled around the people migrating east on Washington. It forced them to the north side of the street giving a wide berth to in front of the Nevada House.

As he lingered near the tunnel's entrance in the middle of the street from the Nevada, Cromie's eyes widened as a wisp of smoke followed a dart of fire. It formed into a solid column that twisted and writhed throughout the building. Then the north wall of the Nevada Hotel collapsed, exposing each of its seven floors. Each bed and wall was on fire. Every room and secrets revealed to the world a moment before they went up in threads of smoke. Hot tears streamed down his face.

Then its brick façades blackened and fell apart bit by bit. Windows panes cracked and glass shattered on the seven stories of the boxlike structure. Intense heat dissolved mortar. It looked like a one hundred-square-foot ice cube melting among glowing bricks and blocks.

Cromie felt Avers' hand on his shoulder.

"Everything I had, everything I owned was in there. My neighbors. Everyone there," Cromie choked from emotion and smoke. Words failed the stalwart journalist.

Avers wanted to be sympathetic. But he recently met this man and didn't know what could provide comfort at a moment like this.

A man wrapped in a blanket ran up to Cromie. He looked younger than Cromie. His eyes were wild but his manner stiff. They acknowledged each other with a nod.

"Bross is on his way," he said. William Bross, former Illinois Lieutenant Governor and co-owner of the Chicago Tribune, also owned the Nevada.

"There's nothing he can do," Cromie responded as if he was told the sky was blue.

"The Garden City House burned like a box of matches," he said. "East and northeast it looks like a surging ocean of flame. Iron pillars melted like warm butter." Then just as quickly he scampered off north.

"His name's Chamberlain. He's a reporter with the Chicago Evening Post," Cromie said matter-of-factly. Despite the tears, his expression remained vacant.

Avers remembered Cromie mentioning his name before by the O'Leary fire after he returned from Goll's shop. He wondered how long ago it was. Time had become irrelevant.

A pillar of smoke and heat rolled over them. It stirred Cromie out of his stupor of self-pity. He took in his surrounding as if for the first time. The realization that they were standing in the middle of a fire awed Cromie. Buildings on both sides of the street were burning. The stench of charred wood and flesh encircled them. Another fire devil formed.

"Let's get out of here!" shouted Cromie and joined the flow of people east toward Lake Michigan which was about a mile away.

"The Nevada," Cromie spoke fondly. "A lot of newspaper men lived there. Theater people too."

Avers and his fellow travelers urged Cromie eastward with the trunk-laden wheelbarrow.

"Now everything I own is in that trunk," Cromie gestured weakly at the giant suitcase. "These are all the clothes I own." Spreading his arms, he displayed the dirty, ripped, burnt gray suit jacket and pants. Patches of soot spotted his clothes as well as his shoes, grayed with dirt and grime.

"Did you notice?" Cromie said to the silent Avers. "Did you notice? There's no fire men here. No police either. It's every man for himself at this point!"

Cromie sympathized with the desperation and fear in the eyes of his fellow travelers.

Just west of LaSalle Street, Booth was fascinated by a prosperous-looking man lowering items by rope one-by-one to three men in spotless vests. He assumed they were most likely servants. All around the man on the third floor were windows with flames shooting out. He stood by as he slowly let down bags of clothes, silverware, a clock, money and a basket filled with an odd assortment of valuables. One by one each item descended from three floors above. The item was retrieved by one of the men. Then the rope would retreat back inside the window.

"Aren't you afraid of being burned alive?" Booth shouted. He asked merely out of curiosity. He had no true concern for the man's safety.

"Now don't fret for me, my friend. That is my stairway." He said dangling the rope.

Booth thought it was rather presumptuous for the man to consider him a friend.

A set of books were let down. Booth was mesmerized as the rope slithered its way back up.

Then a yelp and the rope dropped down again but this time nothing was tied to it. The rope wiggled a bit. The man slid down as flames formed a wreath around the window pane he just exited.

Naturally, the rope burned away. The man dropped about ten feet onto the sidewalk. He scrambled over to his belongings cradling his arm. He made sure his money was safe.

"I have enough money for a doctor," he grinned at his friends.

He looked around and noticed the rope and the man who asked about his safety were gone.

CHAPTER 19

A young man walked beside Cromie with a friend. Both wore unburned and clean clothes.

"I'm suffocating!" he gestured dramatically at the smoke floating overhead.

"Let's go home then. We've seen enough," his friend said.

Cromie stared at them. "You've seen enough?" he asked amazed at the casualness of their conversation.

"We just came over from the other side of the river to see what was going on? We're just sightseeing."

Cromie's eyes widened and his jaw dropped. He wanted to attack these men and actually suffocate them. He took one step toward them and stopped.

Cromie's head twitched hearing something above the roar of the fire and whistling of the wind.

Avers strained for a moment then could also distinguish the deep clanging of a massive bell versus the sharp pinging of the fire engines.

Cromie swiveled around. "The Courthouse bell."

"Dear God in Heaven," Cromie groaned. Now he pointed east.

"The Courthouse. The Board of Trade! It's an inferno over there!"

The fire moved from Conley's Patch to City Hall.

He unlocked the trunk and pulled out his camera.

"We need a photograph of this! I still have a job to do!" Cromie yelled because the roar of the fire devil and the creaking of fleeing horse carts split the ears.

"Booth is heading east. I saw him. We need a photo of him," Avers shouted back.

Now going with the human surge, Avers and Cromie made good time proceeding to the Courthouse two blocks away.

The Courthouse cost an outrageous one million dollars to build. Its west wing housed offices for various municipal departments including the mayor and the Police and Fire Board as well as the fire alarm telegraph. The Cook County offices, courtrooms, and county records were located in the east wing. The county jail was in the basement.

Expectedly so, it stood taller than the average building in Chicago. To increase to its impressive stature, a two-hundred-foot tower and cupola rested on top of the three stories tall.

Also, the Courthouse was considered to be the most flamboyant. It integrated marble and limestone with arched pediments above the doorways and ornamental balustrades around the balconies and roof.

Ironically, firemen of the steamer named Chicago aimed torrents at those ornamental balustrades. The hose attached to the hydrant at Clark and Washington lacked the force to reach the roof three stories above.

The firemen could see some movement above despite the lateness of the hour. More than forty feet in the air, scurrying figures carried water buckets and brooms around the cupola in the dark. They dumped water and beat sparks and embers meandering down from the southwestern sky. In the darkness, those sparks and embers lit like beacons for their own destruction.

One of the men was the tower watchman, Mathias Schaefer. Like the others, his clothes and whiskers repeatedly caught fire. He smothered the sparks with the slap of his hands while trampling tiny flames on the

Courthouse roof.

That was until a red hot piece of pitch caught his eye. He guessed it to be the size of his hand. It sailed over his head and, by happenstance, maneuvered itself between the broken panes of a window under the cupola. By chance, it landed in a pile of wood shavings left unswept from the clock repair.

Almost immediately smoke emerged through the same broken pane. Schaefer smelled it before he saw the first snippet. He alerted his fellow smoke eaters. He joined the men to the north side of the roof. They descended through a door under the balcony. He turned around the night operator for the fire-alarm telegraph who was going up to help. One of the last men to follow Schaefer was his assistant, Denis Deneen.

By the time Deneen reached the exit door on the roof, fire blocked the stairway and heated the iron. Smoke overflowed the area between the door and the top of the stairs. Knowing he had very little options, he slid down the iron banister. He burned his hands and scorched his whiskers on his way down.

The main fire bell rang continuously throughout the building.

As they made good their escape, they shouted warnings for everyone at each of the five floors. They performed a quick search on each floor and in both wings. They set the Courthouse alarm to ring continuously. In the telegraph operator's room, they saw flames crack through the ceiling. Plaster dripped like melted butter. They shut the fire doors on each floor.

When they reached the ground floor, the firemen and Courthouse workers exited through the west wing. All except Schaefer exited.

Deneen sought first aid.

The night telegraph operator donned a helmet and joined the fire crew of the Titsworth.

Schaefer continued to the basement to give a head's up to Deputy Sheriff Ed Longley. Longley was not alone. He was known for associating with the criminal element of, not only Chicago, but all of Cook County. Longley was the jailhouse guard on duty.

Avers and Cromie arrived in the middle of organized chaos southwest of the Courthouse.

To their left, smoke wafted off the roof of the Merchant's Building, Sheridan's Headquarters. Enlisted men worked side by side with officers removing whatever U. S. Army records and gear they could. They loaded up Army wagon after Army wagon.

Across the street to the south, men ran into the Union National Bank with small barrels. Police officers dispersed crowds.

Cromie clicked a photograph quickly. His adept fingers focused, clicked the shutter, and removed the plate smoothly while uniformed men bustled about him. He wrapped the plate in the soft, black cloth and shoved it and the camera back inside the trunk.

As the police officers cleared the street, Avers and Cromie couldn't believe their eyes. Who should they see standing kitty-corner on LaSalle and Washington but Booth.

Just milling around the burning Board of Trade was Booth. He was wrapping up a length of rope that he just stole and admired the fire erupting at the top of the Courthouse.

At first, Cromie interrupted the soldiers from hauling stacks of papers.

"You need to arrest that man," he said pointing to a dapper looking gentleman with a coil of rope around his shoulder.

Avers heard his Army buddy shouting orders. Hoping for the best, he spoke up. "Booth is standing across the street."

"I don't have time for this, Phil," Campbell said and commanded his men to move faster.

One of the soldiers pulled away from Cromie. "I have my orders and they're not from you."

Turning to Avers, Cromie suggested, "Let's get one of those cops."

"You really think they'll believe us?"

"It's absurd how close the Army and cops are to him! He's right there."

"Look around. We're in the middle of absurdity."

Gathering their wits and determination, they accepted the fact that they would have to capture Booth themselves. Then hope someone would believe them in the midst of all this madness. They focused on their mission to apprehend the villain.

Avers and Cromie slowly advanced upon on Booth who was transfixed by the Courthouse fire. Mere feet away, they were about to swing on him when the building to their right exploded.

CHAPTER 20

James H. Hildreth, Civil War veteran and former 7th Ward Chicago alderman, still harbored a desire to return to public service. He slept comfortably next to his wife with dreams of regaining his former glory when she shook him.

" ... MEN RAN INTO THE UNION NATIONAL BANK ... "

"James, wake up!"

He opened his eyes and saw what he thought was dawn breaking through the eastern window.

"Feels like we just went to bed," he grumbled.

"We did!"

He jumped out of bed and to the window. Pushing the curtain aside he stared at what he suspected were flames a few blocks away. He heard fire alarms and saw a fire engine speed by his home on Halsted Street.

A sly grin spread across his face.

"We got to do something. I've got to do something!"

Hildreth stumbled around and started to put pants over his night clothes. His wife stopped him. She, then, pointed to a vest, shirt, and suit pants laid out for him. Soon he would be ready to be of service to Chicago once again.

When he was fully dressed he sent a boy to deliver a message to a political ally, an assistant city engineer of the Chicago Water Department.

Hildreth arrived at the scene of the fire within the hour. At this point, five shacks on the north side of De Koven were on fire.

He scrutinized the fire fighters as they did their work. He decided it wasn't enough. He stood back and gloried in the blaze. He more gloried in the opportunity this presented to him. Spreading his arms wide as if to encompass the flames, Hildreth bellowed orders to idle people to disperse and clear the area.

Walking around dispersing the crowd, Hildreth spied Chief Fire Marshall Williams and strode up to him.

"It's blowing a pretty good gale, isn't it, Chief Williams!" Hildreth said stating the obvious.

Williams closed one eye and looked down to the former alderman. He recognized the man with the wispy hair and trimmed mustache.

"You should move some of those engines to the north side," Hildreth huffed.

Williams took a deep breath and calmly responded. "My men are doing everything they can. When they put one out, another pops up."

Hildreth found this response unsatisfactory.

"If I may," he began.

"Look up there. You understand the wind is blowing live embers overhead. Beyond the men's reach."

Hildreth opened his mouth.

Williams held up a hand to allay Hildreth. "Sorry, sir, if you excuse me," he said as he hurried over to the other end of the street.

To Hildreth's pleasure, Joseph A. Locke, the assistant city engineer of Chicago, rode up in a carriage. He was the man to whom Hildreth sent the message.

Locke hopped out and sent the carriage away. They exchanged cordial greetings.

"We just can't sit back and do nothing, Joseph," Hildreth said.

Locke nodded. He suspected that Hildreth had some sort of plan. The former alderman's natural leadership quality inspired people to follow his lead, especially if it offered the possibility to enhance one's career.

"This fire is getting out of control. Unless we do something like tearing down some of these buildings. Maybe blast them or something," Hildreth said. The dramatic impact of his fire stopping suggestion would make people take notice.

"You know what a fire break is," Hildreth added.

"Of, of course," stammered Locke.

"Good, follow me. Perhaps the presence of a prominent city official such as yourself will encourage Williams to take more decisive action"

Both men jogged over to Williams. They interrupted a foreman providing Williams with another bleak update.

"Chief!" Williams butt in. "A word, please."

Williams annoyed at the stalwart man. "In a moment."

"Perhaps. I need to introduce myself."

"I know who you are, Mr. Hildreth."

"Well, it is my pleasure to introduce."

"I am acquainted with Mr. Locke as well."

"Then you understand that we don't have time to waste, Chief Williams. We need to create some sort of fire break to stop the advance of this fire. Demolish a building or two. I could gather a thousand men to tear some buildings down. But dynamiting them would prove to be much quicker and more efficient."

"Just, just a short line of buildings at the most," Locke added.

"I have neither the authority nor the means to do that, Mr. Hildreth. And, more to the point, neither do you," said Williams hoping to end the conversation.

"Of course, I abhor the thought of destroying private property as well. But for the public good!"

Williams knew he would not be rid of these meddling men unless he acquiesced.

"Listen, if you locate the appropriate amount of explosives and get approval from the mayor, I'll consider it," Williams said exasperated.

"Good show," Hildreth said cheered up at the prospect.

Hildreth and Locke, excited at the opportunity to perform this heroic public service, needed to find a method to expedite travel to the Courthouse. He knew City Hall occupied upper levels and kegs of gunpowder were locked away in the basement level.

Williams was relieved to see them run off on what he was certain was a fool's errand.

Near the scene on Canal Street was another compatriot of Hildreth. Having been an alderman he was acquainted with a great many persons of influence.

Benjamin Bullwinkle was the superintendent of the Fire Insurance Patrol. The Chicago Board of Underwriters formed this unit less than a week previous. It had limited authority during an actual fire. But most importantly, it had a wagon. Bullwinkle was accepting "donations" of five dollars per trunk to haul personal belongings to safety.

Hildreth signaled Bullwinkle's attention. In an effort to confront Bullwinkle he almost collided with some fool with a camera.

"You can do more good," Hildreth beckoned.

Bullwinkle rolled his eyes.

Coming closer, Hildreth witnessed an exchange of coin between Bullwinkle and a man with his hand on a burned crate.

Bullwinkle smiled and nodded at the man who dashed off before Hildreth could identify him.

"This inferno is getting out of hand. If we don't do something, it could become the greatest fire Chicago has ever known," Hildreth exclaimed pointing back to the activity behind him.

Only too familiar with Hildreth penchant for hyperbole, Bullwinkle responded with a wave of his hand to the back of the wagon, "James, I really can't help. No hoses or axes on board."

"We need to gather gunpowder and fuses," Hildreth emphasized.

"The wagon is already filled, loaded," Bullwinkle countered.

Hildreth leaned in and whispered, "Take myself and Mr. Locke to the Courthouse and I will deny seeing your transaction and, indeed, even knowing your name, if asked."

About an hour later, Hildreth and associates arrived at the Courthouse. They made a side trip at Bullwinkle's suggestion. He knew of where two magazines of gunpowder were stored. Since neither Hildreth or Locke knew if the quantity of gunpowder stored by the police department in the basement would be enough to satisfy their plan. They agreed.

Unfortunately, the magazines were a half-mile northwest of the Courthouse next to the Chicago River's main stem. The men had to break into the poorly guarded military storage units at State and South Water Streets. They confiscated 2,500 pounds of gunpowder.

At first, Hildreth decided to forego the mayor's permission. He was confident the mayor would support the urgency of the situation.

By the time the wagon reached the Madison Street Bridge, the fire clearly advanced beyond De Koven Street. It showed every sign of approaching the Adams Street Bridge, the next bridge south of them. Pieces of flaming debris hovered aimlessly like fireflies in a cloudy night two blocks away.

In the wavering orange glow of the South Side fire, Hildreth could barely make out two men with a trunk pass over the other bridge with flames on their heels.

All of them agreed it would be foolhardy to ride into a strong wind over bumpy roadways through fiery neighborhoods with such a load. The night sky was lit up with drifting embers and floating sparks.

The wagon full of explosives retreated through sparsely occupied streets to the Courthouse. Soon those pathways would be gorged with humanity.

With the help of police officers, Hildreth, Locke, and Bullwinkle unloaded the small kegs of gunpowder. They locked it away in the basement trial room.

Bullwinkle left with the wagon to "assist" the growing number of citizens in need.

Hildreth and Locke went to the municipal offices to get authorization to create the fire break.

"We, we don't need the mayor," Locke said. "A fire or police commissioner can issue an order. Even a judge will do."

Hildreth considered it and agreed.

Entering the main offices of City Hall, they were pleased with the bustle of activity within.

"I need to speak with a fire commissioner," Hildreth asked the smartly dressed man at the front desk.

"None are in the office at the moment," the smartly-dressed man said punctiliously.

"Please may I speak with a police commissioner, then?"

"None are in the office at the moment," the smartly-dressed man repeated.

"And the mayor?"

"Not in the office either."

He was bout to inquire about a judge when Mayor Roswell Mason wandered in the outer office conferring with his son, Edward.

"The latest report is the South Side Gas Works is on fire and will blow up," Edward said.

The mayor slumped his shoulders. He was finishing his uneventful two-year term, now this.

Hildreth strutted into the mayor's face. "I have a solution, Mr. Mayor," he announced.

Mayor Mason sighed in exasperation.

"What is it, Hildreth?"

"We need to adopt some course of action to impede the progress of this conflagration," Hildreth declared.

"It's just us, Hildreth. No one to impress with a speech," Mayor Mason spat out.

Undaunted, Hildreth continued. "You need to issue an order or proclamation for the creation of a fire break."

"A fire break?"

"We can do this immediately, at your authorization. We have commandeered enough gunpowder to begin immediately!"

The mayor nodded to his son who ran out off the office.

"Make it incumbent, a call upon the people, if you will, to demolish a series of buildings to stall this disaster," Hildreth elaborated.

The mayor snapped his fingers and the smartly-dressed man handed pen and paper to him.

He scrawled on the sheet of paper. As he finished, Edward escorted an official looking man to the mayor's side.

"This is an order to sanction this man to organize a fire break with the use of explosives. Please sign it, judge," Mason handed it to the official looking man.

Judge H. G. Miller whispered a few changes in the mayor's ear. Mason altered the order and the judge scribbled his name on it.

Mayor Mason then emphasized, "Under the specific direction of Fire Marshall Williams!" looking Hildreth directly in the eye.

"I will. Give it to me quick," Hildreth beamed.

"Locke is to remain here with me in case I need his assistance," the mayor said insisting on getting in the last word.

Hildreth rushed out of the Courthouse. He could see the fire in the sky but still not touching the Courthouse.

Anticipating the impending Courthouse blaze, two fire engines lined up on Randolph Street.

Not hesitating, Hildreth approached a harried and singed fireman to ask if Fire Marshall Williams was onboard one of the engines. At first, he ignored Hildreth to connect a hose to a fire hydrant.

"I have an order from Mayor Mason himself for Chief Fire Marshall Williams," Hildreth shouted as he held the piece of paper in the firefighter's face.

"The Chief hopped off at an alley on LaSalle," the pipeman said as he tightened the connection.

"Which way?"

"South!" the man grunted with a jerk of his thumb and pushed Hildreth out of his way.

Hildreth magnanimously decided to allow the man the indignity. He was sure the man would feel ashamed later after he learned about what great service Hildreth was about to perform. He imagined the man would probably search him out to offer a humble apology for his rudeness.

These were the thoughts that accompanied Hildreth as he finally located Williams a block away.

Williams leaned against a brick wall in the alley of the Oriental building. He was nursing a burnt hand when Hildreth confronted him.

"Here is a direct order from the mayor. And several kegs of powder at your disposal, Chief Marshall," Hildreth said forcing the paper into Williams good hand. Williams read over the order and relented.

"I don't know where to commence," said Williams surveying the situation. Flames could be seen crossing Madison Street just south of where they were standing. He knew that a block west fires were starting.

"The Union National Bank lies directly in the path. It's only a couple of stories but should be an effective fire break," Williams directed.

"Where's the Union National Bank?" Hildreth asked.

"Right over there," Williams pointed and Hildreth was off.

"The Union Building?"

Williams nodded.

"Be sure you have all the people out when you do," Williams shouted to the back of Hildreth's head.

The building roar of the fire and clanging of additional steamers drowned out Williams' warning.

Hildreth located yet another familiar face from his beloved 7th Ward. The devastation caused by the fire relocated 2nd Precinct Police Sergeant

Louis Lull to the Courthouse.

Chicago Police Captain Michael Hickey of the 1st Precinct assigned Sgt. Lull to provide police chaperons for unescorted women to the safety of Lake Michigan's shores. If one of the women were ill or otherwise physically unable to walk the half mile east, he commandeered a hackney coach.

"Sgt. Lull, the city is in dire need of your services," Hildreth shouted.

Hildreth explained his plan to blow up buildings along Washington Street starting with the Union National Bank. After being presented with the mayor's order, Lull recruited a squad of eight police officers. Lull and two officers cleared the bank. Hildreth directed the others to carry over the kegs from the Courthouse basement. Each police officer hauled a hundred and fifty pounds of gunpowder apiece over to the bank's basement.

Tiny bits of flames could be seen from the Courthouse roof.

Lull ordered the police officers to clear the area. He then met Hildreth in the bank's basement.

After Lull informed Hildreth that the bank was empty, he and Hildreth broke open the kegs. They scattered the powder from one keg to another by the dim gas light inside. Lull measured out a long fuse.

Lull lit the fuse. He and Hildreth ran up the basement stairs and into the back alley. They yelled for all police officers to take cover.

In the back of the Union National Bank, Hildreth and Lull plotted the next target.

In the front of the Union National Bank, Avers and Cromie closed in on Booth.

CHAPTER 21

The explosion blew out the windows and a rear wall of the Union National Bank. The muffled explosion and shattering glass drew the attention of John Wilkes Booth. More specifically the noise caused Booth to turn his head to the left. By turning his head to the left, he saw the blast knock over Philip Avers and Richard F. Cromie. Although he didn't know their names, he recognized their faces.

The building itself did not collapse. The shock wave from the blast was enough to bowl over, but not injure, any unfortunate pedestrian passing by too close. Glass showered them as well.

Booth knew he couldn't draw his gun on them. It would attract the attention of the Army personnel across the street and police officials down the block. He merely ducked into the crowd. He still had his mission to complete.

By the time Avers and Cromie got to their feet Booth was gone. The south and west blocks were vacated of standing people. The Army continued loading wagons on the north. The explosion heightened their sense of urgency. So that only left east for open for Booth's escape route.

They upended the toppled wheelbarrow and trunk. They continued their pursuit in front of the crowd gawking as the Courthouse continued to burn from the top down. They crossed into the Courthouse Square to view the entire southern side of Washington.

Quickly dimming street lights combined with flickering flame at night played havoc with facial identification. Avers scanned and re-scanned the cluster of on-lookers.

Several uniformed men dragged leather mailbags the size of a small cow. They crossed in front Avers and Cromie and obscured their view.

Cromie shouted at the men, "Please, move!"

"The Post Office is like one huge Roman candle," one of the men shouted back. "It was supposed to be fireproof. We're heading to the bridge. If you're smart, you'd do the same." And then they were gone.

"Cromie! Cromie, is that you?" came a voice from the Courthouse Square behind him.

Turning around, Cromie was greeted by a man who gripped his hand.

"Smith? Smith!" Cromie shook hands with him. Smith, similar age and dress as Cromie, was obviously a Tribune colleague.

Avers set down the wheelbarrow.

"This is Philip Avers," Cromie indicated his comrade with the nod. "This is W.K. Smith, Tribune reporter."

"Good. We need more men," Smith said as he gripped Avers' shoulder.

"We're in the middle of something," Cromie interrupted.

"The prisoners in the county jail. They're begging to be released," Smith said pulling Cromie by the hand and Avers by the shoulder.

He hurried them through trees burning like candles to the west side of the building.

"The wheelbarrow," Cromie said.

Avers twisted away from Smith and retrieved it.

"It's all I have left in the world," Cromie told Smith. "The Nevada went up in flames. So did the Post Office. Both were supposed to be fireproof."

Smith grunted. "The Metropolitan Hotel. The place was a fire trap.

Collapsed to a shapeless mass before you could count to twenty," he said feverishly.

Avers wheeled past them.

A group of six bareheaded police officers stood at the bottom of the stairs of the Courthouse. The wind had grown so strong that except for the heavily weighted firemen helmets and women's hatpins no hats remained on heads.

Capt. Hickey was addressing them. He was holding a piece of paper.

A vent in the west wing wall burst into flame. Hickey ordered a young recruit to put it out. Off he went to the side of the Courthouse.

Cromie, Avers, and Smith ran up to the policemen.

"We're here to help." Smith said.

"What?" asked Hickey.

"With the prisoners. I heard them screaming to be let out," Smith answered.

"Good we can use all the men we can get! Like I told these men, since there's no hope of saving the building, I'm ordering the jail cells to be unlocked," Hickey said. "Let's go!"

"My wheelbarrow!" Cromie stopped. "It's all I have left!"

Hickey pointed to an overweight officer. "You. Guard that thing."

Hickey led the charge up the stairs and through the main hallway. A quick turn and they descended the stairway to the jail.

"I've been worried about these prisoners. About one hundred of them," Hickey admitted to the seven men.

They proceeded through the short hallway. The air grew translucent with smoke. The tumult grew louder the closer they got. Voices blended together. Words were unintelligible but the tone of fear and desperation was unmistakable.

Arriving at the outer door of the jail, Hickey pounded and ordered the door be opened.

"Who's there?" shouted the muffled voice behind the door.

"I am, Eddy. The Courthouse is on fire. It won't be five minutes before this roof will go in.

The locked on jail door opened.

Eddy Longley, the jailhouse guard, handed Hickey a note.

"Here's Mason's order to free the prisoners and escort prisoners charged with murder to the North Side to be locked up again," Longley said.

"Why didn't you open the cell doors!" Hickey demanded.

"Inner door's still locked, sir. I haven't been about to open it since Schaefer warned me," Longley said standing by a five-foot wooden beam.

A couple of other men stood back in the shadows.

"Where did you get that?"

"Does it matter?"

The men picked up the beam, four on each side.

County Commissioner Daniel Worthington, a bald and gray-mustached man, stepped out of the shadows.

"I really must protest, Captain," said Worthington. "Any damage you do with that, that battering ram to any part of this building. The cost will be passed onto you. You, all you men will be financially responsible for the damages!"

"Get out of the way, Worthington."

"Can you hear those men inside?"

"Sir, must I remind you that this is a fireproof building?" Worthington told Hickey.

"The Post Office, the Nevada. All fire proof. All gone," Cromie said.

"Now, stand aside," Smith added.

"Under whose authority, sir," Worthington said as a last ditch effort to prevent unnecessary destruction to public property.

Hickey paused. Worthington was renowned for his honesty and his fiscal responsibility.

Then the wailing behind the locked door and wind from outside resounded in the basement room.

"All due respect, Worthington. Move!" Hickey shouted. "On three, gentlemen. One. Two. Three!"

The men started ramming the beam against the steel door. The banging on the steel door quieted the prisoners.

After a couple of minutes, the hinges on the door started to give way. Heartened by that their efforts were working, they rammed the door harder.

On the fourth ram, the door frame gave way and crashed to the jail floor.

Longley went to work unlocking the cell doors.

Longley had a list identifying each prisoner and their charge.

The prisoners filed out one by one as the cell doors were unlocked. Some covered themselves with jailhouse blankets. Hickey and two officers secured the prisoners charged with murder.

Storm of sparks showered out of the vents.

Those waiting to be released paced back and forth. A few banged on the bars to speed up the process of release. The increasing smoke and sparks terrified them.

Prisoners and police led the way out of the Courthouse. The main hallway was encased in flames. Both police and prisoners felt their coats or blankets on fire.

Outside noise from the wind and fire engines further frightened the prisoners.

Smith, Avers, Cromie, Worthington and Schaefer followed the first group of prisoners out to Randolph Street.

On the way out, they ran into William Hawkins Hedges, head of city sewer department.

He was pushing a loaded two-wheel cart filled with plats and surveys from his office.

"Worthington, I've told your men to gather whatever county records they can," Hedges said.

"This building is fireproof," Worthington warned despite the obvious evidence to the contrary. "Return those records."

"Suit yourself. I'm taking these to the LaSalle Street Tunnel," Hedges said exiting the north door of the Courthouse.

They followed Hedges out to a street filled with fire engines.

One prisoner fainted from relief upon stepping foot in the Courthouse Square.

Another wandered around the Square in a daze.

Most ran for safety. Across the street, a jeweler was distributing his wares to anyone who wanted one. He was not going to let the fire claim them. The awning above him read, "A. H. Miller Jewelry." One wagon was trapped between fire hoses. Fire men would not allow them to drive over it for fear it may burst.

Miller seeing the newly released prisoners thought it'd be great fun to invite them to take whatever they wanted.

"Released from jail and given jewelry. This must be what Heaven's like," said a prisoner who filled his pockets with rings, bracelets and necklaces.

Cromie eyed the jewelry hand out and walked over. He grabbed a handful off the wagon and shoved them in his pocket. It might be enough for food and shelter when this was all over.

He stopped when a bluster of wind sound like flapping of sails above his head. The wind carried a sheet of fire over them to a block of buildings across from the Courthouse. Wind hurled cinders and started a fledging fire on the jewelry store's awnings.

The main firefight was centered on Randolph Street to the north and Clark Street on the east. The firefighters' method was to dump water all over the area.

Williams climbed on the Washington hose cart to look for the steamer Coventry for Miller's jewelry store. He was unaware that the Coventry left to go north for repairs. The broken valve attachment to hydrant cracked.

The wind picked up. It caught a fireman off guard and he clung to a telegraph pole for stability.

Smith, Avers, Cromie, Worthington and Schaefer stood on Randolph and looked upon the Courthouse.

Schaefer saw Fire Marshall Williams directing the steamer Economy which was hosing down Sherman House.

Seeing Schaefer, Williams asked, "Weren't you off duty at eleven?"

"Yes, sir," Schaefer said, "But I couldn't leave. The wind, mighty strong wind was blowing firebrands onto the tower. Me, Dennis Deneen, and other watchmen was stamping out fires up there. For God's sake, we were even patting our clothes that caught fire. Then a flaming log crashed through one of the cupola's window. The whole thing went up in flames." He rubbed his scorched whiskers.

"What happened to your hands?" Williams asked.

"Coming down the banisters. Smoke blocked the stairs. The railings were iron. Deneen was the worst," Schaefer smiled.

"What about the prisoners?"

"Hickey released them," Schaefer said. "The murderers were handcuffed and sent to the North Side under guard."

"I know you're off duty, Mathias," Williams said regretfully. "I hate to impose but those boys over there could use your help."

"As long as I'm needed, sir." Schaefer said as he ran down the street to help the crew of the steamer Economy fight the fire starting in the Sherman House.

Cromie and Smith looked at each with a wistful grin.

"Should make a hell of a story tomorrow," Smith said.

"Especially with my photographs," Cromie said. Then his face changed. "Philip, my trunk!"

Both of them ran to the west side of the burning Courthouse. The wheelbarrow wasn't at the base of the steps.

"Damn it!" Cromie shouted.

"Over here!" yelled an overweight policeman near Clark Street.

Ducking the rapidly spreading fire, Avers beat Cromie to the wheelbarrow.

"I brought it over here. I figured it was safer away from the fire," said the overweight officer.

" WHAT HAPPENED TO YOUR HANDS ? "

"Good thinking, man," Avers said as he grabbed the arms of the wheelbarrow.

Cromie caught up and threw himself on the trunk.

"Thank God!"

He opened the trunk and set up. Within a minute, he slid in a plate, focused, framed, and clicked a photograph of the burning Courthouse. As he packed the plate and camera away, Avers jogged back.

"Where were you?"

"That alley over there. A livery stable caught fire," Avers said. "I unhitched and freed the horses. Got them out before the cork barrels exploded."

Having grown accustomed to Avers' exploits, he asked no more questions.

Avers felt he was actually in Hell. And Booth was the reigning devil. All that was missing was Booth holding a pitchfork.

The overweight policeman relieved of his burden ran over to join Lull and other police officers rip down joists and clapboards of a saloon. They met with resistance from the local citizenry, faithful patrons of the establishment. After the awning caught fire, they relented and even provided the officers with the axes and ropes to perform their task.

"I don't see him anywhere," Avers said dejected. "But I know he's here."

Then they heard Schaefer yell. He let out a bloodcurdling howl with just one word.

Schaefer pointed to the crowd and bellowed, "YOU!"

CHAPTER 22

The mass of people along Washington Street provided Booth concealment from law enforcement and military patrols. Most importantly, the blend of faces and clothing made Booth inconspicuous to his nameless pursuers.

He safely watched them push that wheelbarrow across the street and scan the crowd. Then some fool pulled them away into the Courthouse. Suddenly, Booth wasn't their priority anymore. Rather than relief, he felt annoyed. Didn't they know how important he was?

If it wasn't for the fact that the roof was ablaze, Booth thought, they could go up there for a better vantage point to search for him.

He'd meet up with them later. He had plans for them. Specifically, an idea had been percolating in his mind concerning the reporter with the camera. He needed to bait them.

Booth saw a disheveled blonde-haired young woman leaning against a street post. She was wearing men's trousers and a shoe on one foot with a slipper on the other. What attracted Booth attention was what was either a man's shirt or woman's blouse. It was so tattered and dirty that Booth wasn't certain. Much of her cleavage was exposed. That pleased Booth greatly. She, however, acted indifferent as did the crowd surrounding her. He approached her slowly like one would a terrified cat.

"My dear, may I be of assistance?" he said tenderly.

"They're gone. I don't know," she spoke in spurts.

"My name is John. What is your name, my sweet?"

"Em. My parents call me Em. My brothers and sisters. Them too," she continued.

"Em, what a lovely name. A rose by another other name," Booth cooed. He easily wrapped his arm around her shoulder to provide a sense of protection to her.

"What's happening?"

"Minor retribution, my girl. Nothing to worry your pretty little head about."

"Is, is my fam-family?" she stuttered.

"They're fine. In fact, it was they who sent me," Booth said as he slid the rope off his shoulder.

The girl didn't react. She was in shock from seeing her family die in the flames of a hotel. A family of five burned alive in some forgettable hotel. They were all here for her wedding. Shock resulted in amnesia of the ceremony and her new husband. She didn't see him die, just a room collapse around him.

"We're, we're visiting Ch-Chicago for the first time," she stuttered.

Booth led her north and she followed, completely void of sense.

"Sounds delightful. Where are you from, my sweet?" Booth asked oozing with practiced tenderness from years of performing love scenes on stage.

A honey-colored rattail of hair slipped into Em's face. She knitted her thin eyebrows together. Color drained a little more from her well-formed face with a smudge of soot on her cheek.

"I, I don't know," she uttered.

"That's all right. Allow my humble self to protect you, my darling Em," Booth tenderly whispered to her. "You're quite lovely, my fair Em."

A look of confusion brushed her face then the vacant stare returned, "Th-thank you, sir." Booth chivalrously slid his suit jacket around her.

All the activity at the Courthouse kept the multitude along Clark Street focused so Booth could tie the rope under his suit jacket and around the traumatized Em's waist without anyone's interference.

"This is for your protection, Em. So we don't get separated," Booth cooed sweetly.

"Y-yes," she said. The word came out mechanically.

They reached the corner of Clark and Randolph. Booth and Em seemed impervious to the developing wind and near-unbearable heat. Booth tried to locate the men who were chasing him. The crowd along Washington Street had dispersed and were now seeking safety themselves. In minutes, the fire invaded the area.

To the southwest, the top two floors and the roof of the Courthouse were completely encased by flames now. The street to the west of Booth overflowed with fire men, equipment, and engines. Water muddied the streets and fire cascaded the sky.

The third floor windows of the Sherman House at the northwest corner brightly flickered from inside. After ten successful years of being reputed as the most luxurious hotel in Chicago, it would be shut down this night.

To the east, the two-story wooden toy soldiers that adorned the front of the Col. Woods Museum, a well-respected freak show, resembled gigantic blackened torches. All the oddities within like mummies and skeletons were fated to be lost forever.

To the southeast, Booth was unaware but would have taken a certain morbid pleasure that the second fire he instigated claimed a victim of his again. The deceased wife of John Develin was being prepared for burial at Wright's Funeral Home. She was the woman's whose husband cried on Canal Street the morning before. She had a sprained ankle and could not escape the fire on Saturday by Lull and Holmes. Nothing would be left of the corpse for Develin to bury.

Booth stood at the corner waiting for some sign of the two men. Resisting the push of the scared masses, he didn't worry. God had chosen him to provide the divine retribution and would protect and guide him.

Then he heard a bloodcurdling howl of an accusation of "YOU!"

The watchman from the roof identified him.

A smile crept across Booth's face.

Schaefer's yell alerted Avers and Cromie. They followed the direction in which Schaefer's finger pointed.

The vile contempt in Schaefer's eyes matched what Avers and Cromie felt in their hearts.

For a moment, Schaefer impulsively considered grabbing a fire hose and pointing it at the man. Rationality prevailed because the man was in the midst of innocents and the water was vitally needed elsewhere. He would not waste water on the likes of that scum.

Avers shouted to Schaefer, "We'll get him." That gave Schaefer some comfort as he re-focused his attention to fighting the blaze climbing down the Sherman House's rooms. Long scarlet curtains unfurled out the windows and caught fire.

Avers ran ahead of Cromie who had the wheelbarrow in tow. He made it to the corner when a series of horse-drawn wagons and carriages cut him off.

Wagons and carts were now becoming a problem for pedestrians. Before people numbered so great, that wheeled conveyances were mired in humanity. Since the desperation intensified, concern for possessions surpassed that of the fate of people's welfare. Every possible method of transport occupied the street, leaving only the sidewalk for pedestrian traffic.

Children and the elderly were knocked over repeatedly and on occasion run over if the driver deemed it necessary. Any one moving slow was considered a potential obstacle.

Drivers charged outrageous prices to transport items and they felt it took priority over safety. Also the quicker they could dispose of cargo, the quicker they could return for more freight at high prices.

Avers waited for an opening to cross Clark Street. A man in a black tuxedo bumped into him. Incensed by the man's incivility, Avers jerked his head. He could instantly see the man bumped into him because he was confused.

"I was watching Theodore Thomas performing with his orchestra. Then everything went yellow with fire. Everybody ran. It struck me how Thomas was different from Nero. One fiddled away while his Rome was burning, the other roamed away as his fiddles were burning." The man gave a simpering laugh and wandered off.

Avers saw another man pull the bewildered man along and guide him away from the fires.

Booth did not leave. It was as if he was waiting for Avers. Then Booth in his best Midwestern accent shouted out about the Ku Klux Klan.

"The Bloody Ku-Klux have done this, knowing us to have been extra loyal. They have burned our city and it is useless for us to attempt to escape, for they will burn us up too!"

No one reacted, much to Booth's chagrin.

A firehose cart pulled into the intersection to block the wagon traffic. A stream of people including three hunded guests recently evicted from the Sherman House flooded across seeking the safe waters of Lake Michigan a few blocks away from the ever increasing flames.

Avers and Cromie moved with them. Avers was not surprised that Booth waited for them. They had something Booth craved.

A wall of people still separated Booth from Avers and Cromie. A human barrier prevented Booth from immediate capture although Avers watched Booth gambol in the streets enjoying the pandemonium like it was demonic music.

Booth did not run from them as they slowly conspired their way closer.

Avers grunted, "He should hang for this!"

"Captured, tried and hung," Cromie insisted.

Cromie and Avers headed east toward the lake with the mob. Angling through the crowd, they were within striking distance of Booth when they noticed he was accompanying a dazed young woman wearing his suit jacket. They maintained their distance.

In one hand, Booth held a rope and it dangled from around her waist. In his other, the Colt pointed at her side. Booth's suit jacket and her tattered shirt barely covered her breasts.

Avers had not expected this. He recalled that Booth had three bullets remaining.

"Let's go to Col. Wood's Museum, my dear," Booth shouted to get their attention again. Annoyed he was not their sole focus. They were close enough to hear him speak to the girl.

"It has paintings of Indians, a pair of mummies, a book that belonged to the founder of the Mormons, a dinosaur skeleton, and display cases of insects of all sorts of shapes and sizes," Booth told Em who was oblivious. "Personally I always favored the panorama of London. The model of the Parthenon is nice too, if you like that sort of thing."

Avers took a step closer to Booth. Booth held the rope and pointed the revolver against Em's side. The girl did not show any signs of resistance. The men and women around them focused only on their own personal safety.

Once again, Booth had the upper hand. If Avers or Cromie moved any closer, Booth would shoot her. She couldn't run away because of the rope. Yelling any type of warning would only incite further panic in the crowd.

"I'm so terribly sorry, my dear. It appears that Col. Wood's Museum is not open for business at this late hour," Booth smirked and proceeded east.

Avers, Cromie, Booth, and Em continued with the deluge of automatons seeking refuge. They relinquished the roadways to the horses and wagons and stayed on the wooden sidewalks. They were numbed to the scorching heat but could still smell it. The gusts of wind help drive them to the lake but also brought orange and red tongues of flames alongside them.

People were screaming or moaning or crying. The mob like lemmings moved to the water. In the middle, Booth gripped his hostage and no one noticed. Each individual focused on their own horrific existence. Facing tremendous losses and still having their lives at risk, men and women trudged east through heat and smoke. The fire showed no signs of abating, with winds urging them further.

As they reached the end of the block, a deafening crash rang from behind.

The bell, that Matthias Schaefer was bragging about just a few hours earlier, crashed to the bottom of the collapsing Courthouse. The bell clanged all the way down as the fire ravaged its tower. The trees in front of the Courthouse and city hall were snuffed out like burnt candles. The west wing of limestone melted. Smoke exhaled out of windows and wall ventilators. Fire from Worthington's "fireproof" municipal building shot one hundred feet into the wind to add another sheet of fire to the Sherman House.

The Courthouse bowed in defeat as it toppled to the ground. Piece by piece crumbled apart and disintegrated. Floor by floor flames swallowed the remaining three stories. It cost a lot of money and it was now only overpriced rubble.

Everyone and everything halted for that second. Avers, Cromie and Booth felt the vibrations of the collapse. Em was still insensitive to her immediate surroundings. Her mind was still lost in the flames that devoured her family. Chicagoans a mile away heard the crash of the bell as it hit the ground. The final toll of the bell split the ears of those closer.

Then just as quick movement resumed.

"Keep your distance for the sake of the girl," he said. The disorientated girl allowed Booth to direct her to the northeast side past a carriage loaded with people yelling names of loved ones.

Avers and Cromie followed. Avers assumed the burden of the wheelbarrow to give Cromie a break.

"The Tremont House is down the block from here," Avers said unemotionally.

"And judging from the direction of the flames. It'll be on fire soon. If it isn't already," Cromie said.

"That's where I was staying," Avers sighed.

"I'm sorry," Cromie said. "Do you want to try and recover anything?"

"No, I don't have much. Carry my money in my belt."

Avers suddenly remembered that he left his hat in the room. He had bought it in Hawaii.

"Still, I'm sorry for your loss."

"So am I," returned Avers. "But all these people and you lost everything or most everything!"

"The Chicago Times Building is a couple blocks south of here. The fools are probably still working just to beat us to an early edition. That's their racket. Trying to beat the Trib. No thought of how to deliver it or who'll be around to read it," Cromie loudly muttered more to himself than Avers.

They walked past two columns of fire as they shadowed Booth and the girl north on Dearborn Street. They could see Booth talking to her but no reaction or even acknowledgement from her.

Searing heat brushed against the side of their faces. Human sounds of sorrow mixed with the crackling and spitting of fire. The scent of human suffering drowned out that of pungent burnt wood.

Avers allowed no more than half a block distance between them. His mind spun ways on how to separate the girl from Booth.

As they meandered in the mob, they faced to the hotel Avers was staying at.

The Tremont House was untouched by fire. Its neighboring building was engulfed. Awnings burned. Windows panes blazed. Faceless women and men on the roof cried for help. Determined men raced past with wooden ladders. A sole fire engine battled the block long inferno with one hose. Firemen swore because they were unable to stifle mushrooming flames.

Cromie stopped.

"I need to photograph this!" He stopped and unlocked the trunk to set up the camera.

Booth stopped and looked back.

He led the girl closer to Cromie and Avers becoming a barrier to the flow of the crowd.

"What's he doing?" Booth asked.

Avers ignored Booth.

Ladders meant to rescue burned instead when leaned against the buildings.

Cromie focused his camera. He wanted to capture the expressive faces of the individuals on the burning building with flames in the background. This wasn't for the newspaper. This was for those people. To be remembered no matter what happened to them. Sorrow overwhelmed him.

As he pressed the shutter button, a woman leapt from the roof. She jumped to her death. Rather than succumb to fire, she chose another way to die. Cromie witnessed it through the camera lens. His mind captured the image at the same time his camera did. Although a mere moment in time, Cromie saw the woman, lovely in a dress, barefoot, strawberry blonde hair streaming above her, and a baby in her arms.

"Dear God!" his mind erupted. "She had a baby in her arms!" Clearly she cradled an infant in her arms by tenderness with which she held the wrapped bundle. Its short thick arm reaching for its mother's horrified face. No photograph, no camera could capture the image any sharper than the human mind in that moment.

No words issued out of his mouth. He removed his eye from the camera. Both eyes wide, he glanced over to Avers. The look on Avers' face showed he witnessed the same horrific moment.

"Tell me you didn't photograph it."

"God forgive me, I think I did. I didn't mean to. I didn't want to. It just happened," Cromie squeaked. His throat parched.

"Damn Booth to Hell."

In a state of shock, Avers and Cromie staggered north past the Tremont House with flames erupting from its roof and windows. Neither looked back. Avers pushed the wheelbarrow. Cromie removed the plate and chucked it into the burning hotel. He locked the camera inside the trunk.

At the middle of the next block, a very irate John Wilkes Booth waited with his unconcerned hostage. Seeing his two pursuers approach, Booth led Em north on Dearborn. The gun still lodged in her back with the rope still wrapped around her waist.

To the east, Avers and Cromie listened to the mournful engine whistles on the Illinois Central tracks as they chugged and tugged strings of rail cars away from incineration.

Avers tried to determine if Booth was close enough to throw the knife into his throat. He estimated the distance was too great, the crowd too dense, and Booth could possible use the girl as a last minute shield.

They were in the middle of a steady stream. A dray carrying musical instruments passed them and turned right. A butterball of a dowager barged her way through. A weasel-faced man ripped her sparkling necklace from beneath her double chins and ran back. Despite the expensively dressed matron protestations, no one heeded her. An obvious street urchin slid a diamond bracelet off her wrist and still no one cared.

Even Avers ignored the arrogant fool's indignation.

Someone yelled at the corner ahead. "Brink's Express is offering wagons for free. Young's Line is free too." Those were on Wabash Avenue and in the wrong directions for Avers and Cromie.

Many shifted east to take advantage of the offer. Dearborn Street thinned out considerably. The next block north was untouched by fire. An area free of flame unsettled the wanderers. Wooden sidewalks enclosed wooden homes with wooden fences and wooden storefronts with cloth awnings. All destined to be kindling later this night.

Fiery pieces of wood and cloth glided overhead to the north side like will-o'-the-wisps intent on arson. The dark sky reminded those fleeing the fires that it was nighttime. The fire's perpetual bright light had the disorientating effect of blurring the time of day.

After a block of no fires and cool night air, the roadway ended. The mob still not feeling safe from the red and orange flickering lights behind them drifted either east or west. Fires, however, awaited in either direction.

Booth shoved the girl east on another darkened street. No street signs were posted.

"Where are we?" asked Avers looking at the eerie orange glow in the night sky over Chicago behind them.

Cromie's response was mechanical without any emotion. "The main stem of the Chicago River's just over there," he said indicating north with his head. "I think its Trade Street or River Street. Not familiar with this part of town."

They blindly trailed Booth's lead.

"Do not lose that trunk, my friends. It is the source of my immortality," Booth bellowed. Tears dripped down the girl's emotionless face. Booth sang a bawdy song. Avers and Cromie waited for an opportunity to save the girl.

Avers could smell the river although he was upwind. Two and three-story square freight houses and long lumber yards stretched between them and the river. Each building has its own dock for access for any of the two hundred vessels that traversed the river.

"He's heading to the State Street Bridge!" Cromie said passively.

"Is there any way to cut him off? Get in front of him?" Avers asked.

"No. I don't know. None that I can think of," Cromie shook his head.

"Like I said, I'm not that familiar with this section."

Avers' grew angry at his dependence on Cromie. He wished he had more time for reconnaissance of the waterways. He could sense Cromie was near his breaking point.

Cromie was lost in thought. Seeing the woman leap to her death, profoundly affected him in a manner he wasn't prepared. He'd seen dead bodies before. Guilty men hung. Police and fire men injured in the performance of their duties. But this was some random innocent. Leaping to her death and with a child, an infant, in her arms. His mind boggled.

Lost in their individual thoughts, still they pushed on with the wheelbarrow.

The procession to the bridge came to a halt. A parade of sorts proceeded in front of them. Three creaking drays loaded with prostitutes crossed the bridge. Some were subtle. They blew kisses and winked at the crowd. Others were bold. They bared their breasts and flashed their privates to lewd cheers. Mothers covered their children's eyes although a few boys managed to peak through.

As the last crossed, the throng swarmed the bridge. The bridges' oily timber provided fuel for the embers traveling north. Human lines formed to pass over the Chicago River. Only the center roadway was available for passage. The wooden guard rails were aflame. The grease on girders above was on fire. It was impossible to tell where the point of origin could have been. Pieces of the burning bridge dripped into the river and sizzled.

Invisible noises from falling walls, roar of the flames, shrieking of wind, shouts of men, weeping of women and children, and shrill whistles of tugboats moving ships out of danger reverberated.

Booth turned north onto the bridge leading the girl by the rope. He yanked to make her keep up with him. She did.

Unlike before, inhabitants leaving the devastation for safety now encountered resistance. A crush of impetuous citizens traveled into the fiery business district. Some sought to desperately rescue whatever they could from their businesses. Some were curiosity seekers. More were callous looters and career thieves.

By the time Avers and Cromie made it to the head of the line, a line of young men carrying coffins strode down the middle. An undertaker in a dray hauled a large casket directly behind them. Too many still remained between them and Booth. Wind pushed less sturdy men, women, and children against bridge girders. Cloaks caught fire from an occasion flying ember. Men's hats were blown into the river. Women lost scarves and bonnets if they weren't pinned. Through it all, a bull dog trotted behind its master.

"That's the State Street Bridge," Cromie again nodded involuntarily.

On the bridge west, a railing broke. Those on the State Street Bridge listened helplessly to the screaming men, women, and children. Having plunged into the cold river, the strong current quickly swept the numbed bodies to Lake Michigan. Despite the dimming gas lights and the fiery glow, those crossing fortunately could not witness the floating victims. A mound of clothes covered one man and held him beneath the water. His plea for help smothered.

Demanding attention, Booth shot straight into the air. Wagons sped away. Frightened men and women picked up their confused children and disappeared for cover. Avers thought, "Two bullets left."

Booth and Em did not move from the middle section of the bridge. He shook his head to indicate that Avers and Cromie should not move closer. The man with a gun edged to the burning east side with the young woman close to his side.

He gently slid his suit jacket off her shoulders and she offered no resistance. The wind blew open the girl's tattered shirt and exposed her breasts. No modesty registered with the young woman.

Booth casually slipped his jacket back on and dusted himself off.

CHAPTER 23

"How marvelous!" Booth said with a gleam in his eye. "This will do well for me."

Avers and Cromie couldn't believe what they saw. An animated Booth tightly held the rope like a leash on the young woman. Above him, the bright glow of more fires silhouetted him and his hostage. He stood like he was posing for a portrait. The girl merely slumped with shoulders down, head tilted with her blonde hair drooping over her face.

"It is your profound duty, an honor to photograph me. This would make a magnificent vignette!" Booth exclaimed.

Very few remained on the bridge. Those that did allowed the dangerous maniac with the gun and the half-naked girl a wide berth. Only Avers trudged forward with only the wheelbarrow between Booth and himself.

"Halt, cretin," Booth commanded. "I demand you, journalist, remove that camera from that overgrown suitcase and photograph me now. For posterity!"

This outburst stirred Cromie from his sorrowful reverie.

"What?" he muttered.

If they were closer, Avers and Cromie would have seen Booth's face redden in anger.

"You're a journalist. Photograph me for posterity!" Booth shrieked. The girl did not move as if she was dead on her feet.

"It's not newsworthy," was all Cromie could think of in response.

Avers saw Booth raise the gun to the girl's head. He dropped the wheelbarrow and ran toward captor and captive.

Booth pulled the trigger. He let go of the limp girl and the wind propelled her over the side.

Avers grabbed the uncoiling rope. He braced himself as he heard something splash below him.

Booth giggled and said, "I didn't shoot her. You can still save her. She's still alive. Otherwise she is doomed to suffer the same fate as Ophelia."

The rope was taut. The ointment was wearing off. The gunshot wound in his shoulder dully ached. He remembered the tube was still in his blazer. He had no idea where it was now.

Booth leaned against Avers' ear and whispered, "Let your journalist friend know that I'm going to the Chicago Historical Museum to burn Proclamation 95 to ashes." He escaped once again. Avers once again had to chose between capturing Booth and saving some poor soul that Booth deemed unworthy to live.

Avers dug his boot heels into the red hot metal braces. He could feel Lake Michigan pull the poor girl toward it. His muscles resisted being dragged into the icy river, but couldn't haul the girl up. The drag of the river was too strong, but he refused to let go. The river current was not weakening but his grip was.

Then another pair of hands seized the rope with him. Cromie ignored the wheelbarrow to help Avers save the girl. Then another pair of hands and another joined in the rescue. Several men disregarded their own safety for the sake of the girl.

They tugged in unspoken unison. Five men focused on one purpose.

Through the rope, they became aware that the waterlogged girl escaped the clutches of the Chicago River. Still they heaved the rope hand by hand, length by length. They could sense the wind combat against their combined rescue efforts.

The rope began to smolder from a nearby flaming railing. Another man recklessly volunteered in the rescue effort.

Six men strained inch by inch until the girl's body was within reach. The cross girder underneath trapped the girl.

Four women did not hesitate to brave the burning sides and haul the girl onto the bridge deck.

Avers, Cromie, the men, and the women exhaled. Cromie examined the young lady's condition. No gunshot wound was evident but the girl wasn't breathing at all.

"She's dead," Cromie groaned with tears welling up. He was trying to think of something erudite to say in honor of her but he didn't even know her name. All she had to show for her entire existence, all she had to show for it was the clothes she wore. Men's trousers, a tattered blouse, a shoe and a slipper, dirty, half naked, disheveled, and dead were all the words Cromie could conjure up to describe her.

Avers gently untied the rope from around her waist.

A feeling of futility beset the would-be rescuers. Every experience tonight suddenly felt hollow. Despite their noble, unselfish, risky efforts, this horrible night claimed another.

One of the women solemnly draped a grayish bed sheet around the poor girl's body.

"We'll see she gets a proper Christian burial," she said. "What were the poor dear's name?"

"I don't know," croaked Avers.

Cromie's head shook.

All the men as impromptu pallbearers tenderly lifted her body up and carried her to a wagon laden with home furnishings. Somehow, it wasn't a burden. Laying her down, several made the sign of the cross in hopes that would provide some peace for her and themselves.

One of the men handed mugs to each of the men and poured whiskey in each.

They toasted the young woman's memory. Then the wagon wheels squeaked away to complete its trek across the bridge. The men and women paraded after it in somber silence.

"We're going to need this rope," Cromie said as he walked back to the trunk. "Where's the Chicago Historical Museum?" They left the trunk near the south end of the bridge.

"What?" Cromie look bewildered.

"He said he's going to the Chicago Historical Museum," Avers said as he looped the rope around his good shoulder.

"There is no such place!" Cromie said.

"Damn. He swore he was going to set Proclamation 95 on fire", gasped Avers.

"My God, he would, wouldn't he?" Cromie stared north.

"What's Proclamation 95?"

"Everyone knows it as the Emancipation Proclamation. An original copy of it is in the Chicago Historical *Society*!"

"How far is it?"

"Ontario and Dearborn, probably? About a mile north, I think."

"You think? Aren't you sure? Damn it, man. I thought you knew this town like the back of your hand"

"To hell with you, Avers. This whole town's burning to the ground. People are losing everything. That girl lost everything including her life. I've lost almost everything. Everything I own now is in that trunk. We watched people die." His voice cracked with grief.

Avers hung his head and rubbed his face.

"I'm sorry. Forgive me," Avers said sincerely. "You've done more than enough, Richard. Go find some shelter. I'll take it from here."

Cromie shook his head and shrugged. "No, I'm seeing it through to the end. That Confederate bastard needs to pay. Whatever he's planning on doing."

With Booth and his gun gone, the pathways instantly flooded with every possible transport and pedestrian. Buggies and wagons jostled the seething masses. Horses threatened to trample. Wheels threatened to crush.

A blaring horn echoed between the riversides. The grinding of metal against metal resounded from the center of the bridge. The entire bridge structure vibrated.

"What the hell?" Avers said turning to Cromie for an explanation.

"Run!"

CHAPTER 24

Avers matched Cromie step for step as they bolted to the south end of the bridge where the wheelbarrow was still sitting. Cromie grabbed it and wheeled off the bridge. Avers two steps behind but heard footfalls pass him.

" ...TENDERLY LIFTED HER BODY UP... "

The bridge emptied within a minute. Then it swiveled. The north end swung eastward and the south end swung westward with ear-rattling squeaks and squeals. The entire structure shifted from being perpendicular to being parallel to the river.

A single tugboat towed a hundred-ton brig to the watery protection of Lake Michigan. Its sails were rolled up but the crew was still stamping out fires with wet towels. Tall bare masts and riggings required long rods to extinguish flames that randomly popped high up. Descending embers also charred the crew's clothes.

"This'll take about fifteen minutes," Cromie said relived to be in possession of his trunk again.

Flames merely took a brief respite on vessels in the effort to cross the river and continue the march to the North Side.

Avers and Cromie stood alone amongst a suddenly gathering throng.

Avers asked Cromie. "What do we do now?"

"Wait," shrugged Cromie.

"Let's go to the next bridge over."

"The one down the river is opening. The one up river closing."

Cromie could see the anxiousness in Avers' eyes.

"You've been chasing him for six years. Surely you can wait fifteen minutes."

"I've been this close before and he's gotten away."

Calling over to a wagon driver, Avers asked, "How much to carry us to the next bridge over?"

"Fifty dollars," said the drayman.

Checking his money belt, he grudgingly agreed to the expensive fare. It was most of what he had left but it would be worth it. Cromie and the wheelbarrow walked up behind Avers.

The drayman held up his hand. "Fifty dollars each. And another one hundred for the wheelbarrow."

Cromie shook his head indicating he didn't have the money. "All burned up with the Nevada."

"You thieving bastard!"

"A thieving bastard with a horse and wagon," he grinned.

Avers and Cromie considered forcibly taking the wagon but eyeing the driver's other passengers who paid the exorbitant fare they decided against it. The rate did not vary with the other two teamsters.

"It's his racket," Cromie suggested. "Maybe he lost everything in the fire. Maybe he's trying to provide for his family."

"That would be of some comfort," Avers said at his friend's attempt to lighten his mood. "But I still cannot afford it."

"Go ahead without me," Cromie offered.

"I need you. You know where we're going," Avers said.

"I can give that thieving bastard the address."

"But I don't trust him. I trust you. You're one of the very few people who know Booth's alive and needs to be stopped. I've never had anyone work with me. And we need that trunk to capture Booth."

So they waited for the bridge to swing back.

"Six years?"

"Like I said, Mary and Tad Lincoln were the only other two who knew; who believed me."

A man with thin hair carrying an art portfolio slapped Cromie on the back.

"Rich? Rich, is that you?"

Turning around, Cromie saw the man. Cromie's lips took the shape of sucking a lemon.

"John. What are you doing here?"

"On assignment for Harper's Weekly, of course."

Turning to Avers, the man shook his hand and said, "John R. Chapman, artist for Harper's Weekly. You've probably admired my work in Harper's Weekly."

Before Avers could respond, Chapman turned back to Cromie. "Isn't this incredible? I've already sketched a couple scenes for Harper's. Great stuff. Wait until you see it. A woman and her children on the Randolph Street Bridge. Flames and smoke arcing for two miles. A wall of flame one hundred to two hundred feet in the air. Massive buildings dissolving like the cardboard playthings of a child, dissolving like a mountain of snow. I started drawing everything I saw. I catch the essence of drama, the despair. Great stuff. And it should fetch a pretty penny from Harper's Weekly."

"People are dying, John. People are losing everything. Their livelihoods. Families destroyed. Entire neighborhoods vanished," anger swelled up in Cromie.

"It's our job to let the world know, not to get involved," Chapman sneered.

"We are involved," Cromie shot back.

"Losing your sense of objectivity. Happens to some of us," he har-rumphed and stormed away with his nose in the air.

"It's Richard, not Rich, you obnoxious ass!"

Again the warning horn blared and echoed. Metal against metal repeated its grinding work. The bridge was once again connected the north and south river side of State Street.

Much of its upper timbers were still burning hot. The guard rails had since dissolved completely away.

Avers and Cromie raced the solid stream of movement across.

With the southern half of Chicago glowing brightly behind them, Cromie and Avers fell silent as they finally landed on the north side of the State Street Bridge. Acting with one mind, the extemporaneous duo hiked north along State Street. Saving whatever reserves of strengths remained; they focused on their singular task and did not speak. They did not need to.

Again lumberyards and freight houses stood abreast State Street. Square freight houses up to four stories and wide lumber yards overlapped along the river. Docks dotted the shoreline. The north edge of the river mirrored the south edge.

Avers and Cromie trudged past unmindful of a couple of grain elevators four stories tall.

One block later on Kinzie Street, a fire burst out of the Wright's Stables just to the east of them. Wind formed blazing fingers reaching north. Whatever it laid a finger on turned to flame like whatever Midas touched turned to gold.

Avers and Cromie hesitated. The stable horses whinnied and snorted in alarm. Instinctively, Avers swerved toward the flames. But he heard men releasing the horses. As the horses galloped by, he felt relief and continued his mission.

Two gunshots rang out to the west. Avers and Cromie started in the direction expecting to see Booth. What they saw was a staggering man unloading a pistol into the flames of a grain elevator. A much younger man, possibly his son, placed his hand on the man's shoulder. The older man shook his head and relinquished the weapon to the younger man.

The younger man stepped out into the street. He signaled an oncoming horse and buggy with one shot in the air. The coachman halted the wagon. The younger man and the older man hopped into the wagon at gunpoint and demanded the driver to make haste.

When a railcar filled with kerosene exploded on the tracks, east of State Street Bridge, Avers and Cromie were distracted again. Cromie trembled as the flames stretched up to the night sky. The wooden trestle above the railcar was set on fire.

They heard another rapid series of blasts in another direction. Barrels of oil at Heath and Milligan Manufacturing Co. burst like muskets shots.

The explosions were extraneous. The fire already launched its maiden voyage into the North Side less than an hour ago. Incendiary cinders, embers, and firebrands were directly delivered from the Courthouse.

As Avers and Cromie entered the next block, the North side assumed a mostly affluent residential appearance. Chicago aristocracy resided here. Impressive and expensive mansions of brick and stone intermingled with modest frame homes. Majestic trees like maples, oaks, elms, and willows lined the streets. Stately crabapples, birches, and evergreens roosted closer to the homes. Streets boasted an occasional paved road.

The community despite its prominent stature was not exempt from fire. The opulent distance between houses was countered by decorated yards covered with fallen autumn leaves which piled against wooden fences and sidewalks. The rapidly spreading fire accepted its invitation to visit the prosperous neighborhoods.

Again the whipping wind pushed sparks and embers from house to house, leave pile to dry grass, wooden porches, stables, gardens, and twisting ivy.

Even paved roads offered no impediment to advancing fire. Sparks danced along them seeking somewhere to take hold.

Like the South Side, the fire rained down from the sky allowing scared men and women a multitude of minutes to pack their house into a trunk. They hampered passage in streets and alleys with heavily laden wagons and buggies. Horses were hitched to some. Most carts and wagon were being pulled by hand. Pedestrians lugged what they could or left suitcases on the sidewalks or to be trampled in the street.

Unlike the South Side, the buildings were built yards further back from the street. The walls of flames didn't crush against Avers and Cromie like they did in Conley's Patch.

Another difference from the South Side, Avers noted, was the quality of items being rescued. One woman cradled a marble clock in her hands. A girl hoisted a cat in one arm and swung a caged canary in the other. The canary died from heat and smoke.

They saw members of society hauling fine luggage and fashionable carpetbags, expensive pillowcases and gaudy garment bags. One serious-looking man carried a black valise exquisitely embellished with floral designs.

Roadways, paved and unpaved, were busy with not only horse-drawn trucks, wagons, and coaches, but three-wheeled hand carts, dollies, and other wheelbarrows, mostly pulled by hand.

The same disregard for safety was apparent when a speeding express wagon collided into a store truck at an intersection. No one stopped to assist them. Passersby decided their own carelessness did not merit aid.

Pedestrians remained on the sidewalk unless a sporadic fire obstructed the path.

Another difference was the availability of garden hoses. Homeowners and servants drenched houses and household goods like sofas and tables in the front yards. A coachman in top hat, long coat, and breeches steadfastly doused the side of a mansion with a handy garden hose.

Bits of burning hay from backyard stables and barns would take flight in search of the main house.

Pails and vases of water could be seen being poured out of two-story homes.

As Avers and Cromie passed another block on their progress north, flames dominated. Not content to remain on the upper levels of mansion, a blaze would descend and even pranced out the door.

A yellow bonnet adorned with charred flowers fluttered by Avers. Low-pitched screams and high-toned shrieks for help overpowered the whooshing wind and roaring fire.

"The gates are locked," shouted a bass voice behind a six-foot blazing fence. Other higher-pitched voices wailed and cried out. Former immaculately manicured trees and shrubs burned around a three-story manor.

Avers set down the wheelbarrow. Deadpan, he approached a section of fence not obstructed with fiery flora. He leapt at the fence feet first. Twenty feet of it caved into the yard. A man, woman, and child escaped. Then an older man and woman skittered out a few feet further. Then a maid cleared the burning fence only to have her skirt catch fire as she ran over the sidewalk. Avers, now on his feet, ripped away the maid's skirt and tossed it into the street.

Without a word of thanks, the group hurried along ahead.

Avers assumed the burden of the wheelbarrow and proceeded north.

"That was rather rude of them. No gratitude," Cromie said.

"I didn't do it for their praise. I did it because it needed it to be done," Avers shrugged.

A man with a demented smile jogged past them. He paused and tilted his head at them. In his arms was half of a marble mantle. He joked, "That's all there is now but I'm going to see if I can't find another and build a house to fit it." Then he ambled on.

After covering another block, Cromie looked up at a street sign and let out a chuckle.

Avers glanced over at him.

"We're crossing Indiana Street," Cromie smirked.

"So?" Avers asked.

"That's where I'm from. A little no-name town in Indiana. Rushville, Indiana. Came to Chicago. Knocked around doing odd jobs until I finally hooked up with a job at a newspaper. Been the newspaper racket ever since."

"Always at the Tribune?"

"Nah, it's the third paper I've worked for. Publisher's a fine man. The editors, well, they're a pain in the ass. Demanding but I've learned a lot from them."

Cromie was about to ask where Avers was from when a dark eastbound procession on Indiana made them pause. More coffin carriers plodded along. Bodies wrapped in winding sheets, dead but not yet buried, were stacked on a horse-drawn dray. It was a stark reminder of the poor woman they hauled out of the river and why they were headed north.

Again, they travelled on in silent remembrance.

They remained mute as they passed a man who had just finished loading a buckboard of furniture and linens. A random ember drifted down and the whole wagon went up in smoke. The man just laughed.

The next block, Ohio Street, stirred emotion of a different sort. Two uniformed men balanced a patient in a stretcher. A tousled woman wrapped up in a soiled bed sheet lay peacefully as she held her sleeping baby. The bedraggled father beamed beside her.

"She gave birth minutes before our house caught fire. Mere seconds really," he radiated joy for the future.

Avers and Cromie smiled. One of the uniformed men stumbled but maintained control of the stretcher. The sudden movement jostled the baby.

Avers and Cromie heard the baby cry. Another harsh memory intruded in the brief cheerful moment. The grim reminder erased their smiles.

A man, obviously a reverend by his garb, and his family, wife, two daughters and a son, rested as the new mother and infant passed by.

"Even in the heart of disaster, His goodness shines through and provides us all with a sign of hope," he moralized.

As if in ironic response, a gale snatched the ream of papers out of his hands, swirled them around, and deposited them onto an imposing mansion with even more imposing flames thirty feet from the street.

"Important papers?" Cromie asked as each sheet transformed into smoke and flame.

"My sermons," the reverend said simply as they all proceeded to cross the street.

"Sorry for your loss," Cromie offered.

"Naught to be sorry for, my son. These're all I have left; my gold, silver, and," gesturing to his family, "hope."

Avers and Cromie couldn't help but smile.

One of his daughters nestled an armful of books. She displayed no signs of struggle but the only clean marks on her face were where her tears streamed down.

Cromie reflected a bit and softly asked her, "May I wipe your face?"

The young lady nodded, "If you please."

He plucked out his handkerchief and with tenderness that amazed Avers dabbed her forehead, nose, cheeks, chin, and around her eyes and mouth until all signs of soot and grime were vanquished. He slipped the handkerchief back into his pocket.

With equal tenderness, she thanked him

Nothing more was spoken as they avoided an array of trampled bundles – satin pillow cases with dress shirts, a wax doll, pieces of a jug, shattered china with blue designs—in their path. They quietly encountered another mass of Chicagoans surging east on Ontario Street.

CHAPTER 25

At Ontario Street, they parted ways. The reverend and his family headed east. Avers and Cromie resumed their quest west.

"That was a remarkable gesture," Avers said

"I'm not a hero like you. I didn't fight in the war. Little acts of kindness is about all I'm capable of," Cromie whispered.

"It was what she most needed, Richard."

"I did it because it needed it to be done, Philip."

Grand homes with blazing roofs staggered among dignified shops with flaming awnings. Torrid heat and burnt smells brushed over them. They pushed against the oncoming crowd. Because of the mass of people in the street, they didn't know if they walked one block or two before they realized they were at the door steps of the Chicago Historical Society. The brick and stone structure built as a three-story Neoclassical style design surrounded by a low picket fence and, of course, wooden sidewalks.

The contents inside the Chicago Historical Society welcomed combustibility. Aged books, daily newspapers, thousands of paper pamphlets and manuscripts, battle flags, and oil paintings openly displayed. Large reception area next to a large reading chamber next to a large lecture room encouraged excellent air flow. Its spacious attic served as a storeroom, or in this case oven, for flammable relics.

Chicago Historical Society was hailed as yet another fireproof building, Cromie informed Avers.

Next door to the Chicago Historical Society, a simple one-story cottage ignited. A gust expelled a stream of flame and coated the fence and gate.

Outside, its window casements burned.

Inside, small flames flickered through its six lower four-paned windows. A quick wind whipped around the front of the building and a blast of sweltering heat hit Avers and Cromie.

Avers fended off the blast and spotted the cellar door on the side had been pried open.

"We're too late," croaked Avers. He let go of the handles of the wheel barrow.

"No, we're not," called out Cromie, pointing east.

At the corner on the other side of the street, Booth waved a long black rod at them. In his right, he gripped the Colt with a roll under his arm. The individual travelers and horse-drawn wagons on Ontario focused only on seeking safety rather than pay attention to some fool waving a gnarled club.

"What's wrong with that man?" Cromie asked not expecting an answer.

"He's not a mere actor anymore, Richard. He's a deadly braggart, self-centered maniac. Dear God, he wants us to acknowledge his part in this insane drama. That's his downfall," Avers answered.

Booth spun around and walked west. After two steps, he turned back to Avers and Cromie. He gestured at them to follow him wielding the three-foot club like a baton.

Avers hustled after Booth. A lowing cow with its back scorched trotted next to Avers.

Cromie lifted up the wheelbarrow to accompany Avers. Alongside him scampered a woman with a live hen and another a man pushing a wheelbarrow loaded with a cook stove and a rubber tube.

Booth had almost a full block head start. He took a break at State Street. He wheeled around to make sure that Avers and Cromie were still behind him. He was amused at the site of the odd quartet that followed his lead.

CHAPTER 26

B ooth pointed the stick north and proceeded up State Street. Again he thrust the stick before him like he was leading a parade.

Avers arrived at the corner of State and Ontario Streets. Cromie was about half a block behind him. Avers waited for him to catch up.

"Hurry," Cromie huffing and puffing. "You'll lose him."

"Don't worry. He's waiting for us."

At the corner, happy voices emanated from a bustling saloon. A blissful drunk sat on top of a piano in the middle of the sidewalk. In a sing-song voice, he repeatedly announced, "The fire is a friend to the poor man. Help yourself to the best liquor around."

So that was it, Avers thought, the owner abandoned the establishment to looters and drunkards who claimed it as their own.

A bottle flew out of nowhere and knocked the drunk off his perch. Even sprawled on the sidewalk, he continued to croon his invitation.

When Cromie arrived at the corner, Avers undertook responsibility of the wheelbarrow. Avers was favoring his wounded shoulder.

A block north on Erie Street, Booth grinning urged them on with a wiggle of the club over his head.

"We don't have to rush," Avers said twitching his shoulder. He left the ointment in his blazer. Again he wondered how long ago that little girl ran off with it. He reminded himself it was less than a day ago. He hoped the little girl was safe. His mind drifted to Claire.

Cromie and Avers rambled north. The rest of their impromptu quartet, cow and all, continued east with the rest of the herd.

Again Avers and Cromie pressed against a weaker surge. Fewer bodies and transports resisted them but the same intensity for safety persisted. Faceless men and women occasionally bumped into them.

They were passing through a strictly residential section again. Magnificent Georgian, English Manor, Colonial, and German Baroque mansions nestled among one another. Long wide lawns and yards unfolded with elms, maples, oaks, birches and charming gardens. A mixture of greenhouses, stables and barns, equally opulent, tucked away in back.

Fire did not differentiate these homes from the shanties, shacks, lean-tos, sheds, and huts on the South Side. Roofs were ablaze. Flames crept slowly but determinedly down the wooden surfaces and across sidewalks.

The air was hot and the smell ashen.

Howling winds mixed with the crackling fire to drown out human cries and commands.

Men still challenged the flames with garden hoses and water pails. Servants were on hand to assist.

Battered fire engines, steamers and hose carts staggered throughout the North Side offered weak resistance. Experienced firefighters never encountered any conflagration this extensive in scope.

Avers and Cromie happened by an ornamental water fountain void of water and fish. They shared the roadway with wandering horses and roving cows freed from their confinement of comfortable barns and roomy stables.

A man in a black waistcoat and tie offered them some wine. He apologized for not having any wine glasses available and let them sip directly from the uncorked bottle. Parched, they accepted. The man was determined not to let the fire destroy his vintages. He presented a corked bottle to them but they declined. He slid it back into his winerack.

Halfway up the block, Booth signaled with the club like a beacon and directed them eastward. He dashed down the street amid the spreading flames.

Shortly, Cromie and Avers stood at the same spot that Booth was at less than a minute before. They stared down Erie Street. The flow was east again to Lake Michigan five blocks away.

The fire intensity increased in collaboration with the litter in the mucky street. Newly created nomads kicked away melted candlesticks, blackened plates, and silverware fused together.

The black club rose above the wide crowd to signal Booth's place among them.

Coaches and carriages were few now. Most of the wheeled transportation had hurried to the lake when survival was the only remaining option.

Avers and Cromie meandered through bundles of clothes trampled in the street with soiled pillow cases full of valuables aflame on the burning sidewalks. Beautiful items lay strewn in the dirt like a buttonhook, Italian porcelain, a brass clock, an onyx box, a white loveseat, a English tea kettle and a iron cast stove. Further along they maneuvered the wheelbarrow around a piano with its legs removed, two busts – one of Shakespeare and the other of Rembrandt, a feather bed, a white cherry table, and hand carved bookcase. All of them were charred or still burning.

Flames engulfed a stone mansion with turrets. Besides it, a garden with a gravel path and cement stairs remained untouched.

A well-mannered woman in a long overcoat directed two men in livery attire and a woman in a maid's uniform as they loaded a wide wagon. One of the men clearly slipped two pieces of silverware into his coat pocket. Avers, Cromie and the woman in the long overcoat witnessed the blatant theft. She silenced Avers with the slight shake of her head. She shrugged and continued to provide guidance as to how she wanted her remaining possessions loaded.

Two black ponies drawing a brown and green phaeton charged past them and outdistanced them promptly.

Avers took note of the female travelers walking alongside them. Beautiful women with coal black hands chatted politely with other ladies with dirty faces. None rudely remarked on the others less than pristine appearance. One young woman in riding clothes carried a sleeping baby. Another tear-stained woman held a dead baby close to her chest. Another woman expressed her annoyance that the train of her silk dress was being stepped on. A proper lady pushed a buggy with dresses and coat. A slight man darted from the sidewalk, snatched an overcoat, and leapt over the flames of a fence before anyone could react.

Cromie remained focused straight ahead. He observed a frowning man tightly gripping a small girl's hand as she cried that it hurt.

Still more abandoned treasures cluttered the pathways. Oil paintings, expertly bound books, baskets of gilded dishes, a white wide-brimmed hat with pink roses, silk dresses, a mackintosh, silver spoons, opera glasses, full length mirrors were left behind as the fire's span broadened.

"These people look like a routed army" said Avers.

"They're shadows feeling their way through a tunnel," Cromie added.

A man with a British accent remarked, "Men and women screamed and shouted, ran wildly, crossed each other's paths, and intercepted each other as if deranged."

The club in Booth's hand beckoned ahead.

Avers and Cromie remained on Booth's trail like bloodhounds. As they did, they took in the surrounding area. Flames unceasingly leapt from house to house in a neighborhood of obviously wealthy homeowners. Dry lawns and autumn leaves competed with pine fences and oak gazebos as if to see which could spread the fires faster. Desperate men gathered whatever water containers to toss on the fires. Homeowners directed servants. Housewives evacuated precious belongings beyond the fire's reach. Butlers, valets, and maids crammed furniture and house wares onto carriages. Organized chaos could only be the description that came to mind.

Yellow fire and red heat rendered the evacuation no longer civilized. Mansions emptied in great disorder and excitement. People stopped trying to stay the flames.

Avers and Cromie forced their way along the avenue, littered with even more costly furniture, some with flame still licking them. A woman knelt in the street with a crucifix praying, oblivious to her dress burning. A runaway truck knocked her to the ground. Goods on the truck were partially burning. A man waltzed up to a pile of elegant chairs and tables and held a burning packing board to it until it was completely immersed with fire.

White hot heat melted iron and steel. Stone turned to powder. Marble and granite fried to lime. Precisely trimmed trees exploded from boiling in their own sap.

A voice further up the crowd shouted, "Everywhere dust, smoke, flames, heat, thunder of falling walls, crackle of fire, hissing of water, panting of engines, shouts, braying of trumpets, roar of wind, tumult, confusion, and uproar."

Avers appreciated that denizens of the South Side were not nearly as loquacious as the North Siders. Although he did agree that the fire on North Side inundated one's senses with the nightmarish cacophony.

Cromie witnessed a drama unfold during this part of his trek. A man and a little girl crouched under a burning porch. They were trying to coax their pet out. But, Cromie overheard that it just delivered a litter of puppies and would not leave them. The man finally lifted the little girl over his shoulder and ran away before the porch caved in.

At the next corner, Avers and Cromie scoured the crowd for a sign of Booth. Then to their right a flicker of movement caught their eye.

Booth stood in front of a mansion, waving his black cudgel over his head again. Assured of his pursuers' attention, he casually strode inside the stately manor.

Avers and Cromie once again wheeled the wheelbarrow north. Many fewer people impeded their progress. Fewer personal belonging hindered their pursuit. Ripped carpets, mangled silk dresses, and lacy intimate garments lay ignored in the middle of street.

Halfway up the block, they stood before the east-facing mansion into which Booth ducked. The upper floors of the grand house were ablaze. It sat in the middle of a wide yard with a garden on each side.

Fire devoured the tall barn in the back as cows and horses were safely led out by a distinguished looking man with a black beard and moustache, two dark-haired girls, a towheaded boy and servants judging by the aprons and workman clothes.

Clearly the hay inside was an active catalyst.

One of the children pointed out that the leaves on the lawn were on fire.

Another indicated that the front greenhouse and roof were as well.

The third cried that the veranda around the house was done for.

A servant, possibly the gardener judging by his overalls, informed his master that the water from the garden hoses had stopped.

Unknown to them, the roof of the cream-colored water pumping station was on fire. The slate roof did not burn but the wood underneath did. Despite its decorative battlements and turrets and arrow slits, it was conquered within an hour. The roof collapsed. Its slate rubble landed on and wrecked the pumps. No more Lake Michigan water could be forced out to hydrants or faucets to fight fires.

The bearded man decided the battle was over and it was time to retreat. He directed each person to take the reins of cows and horses and flee to the Sands, a barren section along Lake Michigan, just a couple of blocks east. The man picked up an armload of papers and led the children, servants, and animals past Avers and Cromie, over a crumpled black umbrella on the sidewalk, and around a hair mattress in the street. He paused in front of the brick two-story house with the pristine marble porch across the street. It was undisturbed by fire. He shook his head and moved on.

Avers and Cromie walked up the wooden steps but left the wheelbarrow. Indeed the front porch roof was smoldering as the child said.

Avers retraced his steps down the wooden stairs and retrieved the trunk.

"Why bring that?" Cromie asked, fearing the trunk and its contents could be damaged.

Avers hoisted the trunk. He would not let it go.

"It is key, believe me," is all he would offer as an explanation.

They entered the front door into the majestic foyer. They could see the fire spreading at the top of the shiny wooden stairs.

"Welcome!" Booth bowed grandly from the library off to the right of the foyer where Cromie faltered and Avers set down the trunk.

The fire on upper floors was content for the moment to remain there but the smell of smoke permeated the house.

Avers edged closer as he asked, "I don't suppose you'll come along peaceably to the police."

Booth cackled.

"... A DISTINGUISHED LOOKING MAN ..."

Avers lunged for Booth. He wrapped his hands around the assassin's neck. Booth punched Avers in the stomach. Avers could feel a rib crack and the wind knocked out of him. His grip slackened. Booth immediately swung his fist up into the Avers' jaw. Avers fell down and shook his head.

Booth proudly displayed his fists in front of him.

"Brass knuckles used by Lincoln's own bodyguards," Booth smirked admiring his fist. He picked up the Colt from the desk behind him. "Part of the abhorrent collection from the Museum."

Booth pulled the trigger and shot Avers in the leg. Avers grabbed his thigh.

"Now, sir, if you would be so kind as to photograph this momentous occasion," Booth demanded.

"What?" Cromie asked incredulously.

"Perhaps I should pose like St. George standing triumphantly over the slain dragon," Booth struck a pose with the gun in the air and his foot on Avers.

Avers grabbed Booth's foot.

Booth pulled the trigger again but the Colt was empty and clicked several times in impotent response.

He tossed the revolver at Avers and shoved him back with his foot. Avers fell back. Blood seeped through the bandage on his shoulder. A bruise appeared along his jaw line.

"This is a historic moment, which you need to capture for posterity. That is why I allowed you to accompany me," Booth announced.

Booth picked up the three-foot stick from on top of the desk. The end of the wooden stick was burning now. He clenched a parchment in his other hand like a trophy. He flipped it open.

"Get out your camera, dolt. I'm about to offer your everlasting fame," Booth bellowed.

"This house is burning and you want your photograph taken," Cromie asked again astonished.

Gritting his teeth, Avers said, "His vanity demands it. He wants credit for this, a grand drama of his own design. That's Proclamation 95 in your hand, correct?"

Booth's insane grin widened. "Very astute."

"Take the photograph, Richard!" Avers insisted as his hand rested on the Colt beside him.

Cromie looked at his companion, who merely nodded at the newspaperman. Quickly, he retrieved and set up the camera on top of the trunk.

Booth posed for the camera.

"This walking stick was Lincoln's own. This document is, indeed, the abomination, Proclamation 95," Booth lectured.

"The Emancipation Proclamation," Cromie corrected.

"Property cannot be emancipated, sir!" Booth sermonized. "In the name of freedom, I will destroy this piece of treasonous lies with the cane of a traitor! These items procured from that so-called Historical Museum. Filled with Yankee propaganda. And you will achieve fame for documenting such a momentous historical American event."

Booth proudly displayed the Emancipation Proclamation. With Lincoln's walking stick, half-ablaze, he set the document on fire. Before the parchment was reduced to a cinder, Cromie photographed the horrific tableau.

Booth distracted, Avers threw his knife. So great was the pain in his shoulder that he missed. The knife stuck into a landscape painting behind Booth.

Booth tossed the document aside. "Now you may leave. So I may finish my patriotic duty. I come to bury Caesar, not to praise him," Booth preached as he swung the burning torch around the smoldering room. He placed the torch between the book shelves.

Cromie looked at the painting and then around the library. Recognition dawned on him. Words stuck in his throat.

Booth's mad smile returned as he leapt onto the desk. Both hands spread in the air. He brandished Lincoln's walking stick like a stage prop.

"Yes, this is the home of Isaac Arnold. A self-imposed chronicler of the War of Northern Aggression."

"I met Arnold in '65. He was part of the honor guard for Lincoln's body return to Illinois. I didn't recognize him out in the yard," Cromie said.

With wide eyes, Cromie faced Avers who was still squirming on the floor. "The Tribune did a story on him. He's gathered at least ten volumes of written correspondence. Letters written by Lincoln, Grant, Farragut, Sherman. McClellan, Seward, Sumner, Chase, Colfax. Speeches. State papers. Irreplaceable."

"Irreplaceable," giggled Booth.

"These are important records, significant," Cromie gasped with the air becoming heated and replaced with smoke.

"What could you have against Arnold?" asked Avers getting to his feet.

"Isaac Arnold is one of the 'honorable men' that I spoke of as Mark Antony in 'Julius Caesar' at the Winter Garden Theater in New York in

1864," Booth posed as if still on stage. "He is a traitor, sir. A traitor to his race. A traitor to his class. A traitor to history. A traitor to his country. He is the spawn of America's greatest traitor, Benedict Arnold."

"You're America's greatest traitor," Avers said.

"No, sir, I am her greatest patriot. Destroying its weaknesses. Removing a cancer like Lincoln. Even ending one more of his blood line, that youngster, Tad. Poisoned him to whittle down the chances of the Lincoln brood continuing. Eventually Robert as well," boasted Booth.

"You admit you killed Tad," said Avers as if he was spitting up bile.

"Admit it? I proudly proclaim it before God and country from the highest mountaintop Yes, I poisoned that little shit!"

Something in Avers' mind snapped. Booth ignited his last fire. The fire was in Avers' eyes. All sense of pain drained from Avers' body.

Enraged, Avers kicked the desk from under Booth. Booth fell to the floor as flames erupted along the base of the walls. Avers kicked the torch out of Booth's hand. Booth hurled his body up and swung at Avers. Avers blocked the jab. Balancing on his wounded leg, Avers landed a body blow in the Booth's stomach then an uppercut to the jaw. Booth, winded, swung wildly at Avers. Avers easily dodged the brass-knuckled fists.

"One last chance to surrender," Avers offered but knew and hoped it would be rejected.

Booth reared back his right hand, telegraphing his punch. Another sharp upper cut from Avers knocked Booth against the burning shelves. Booth's suit jacket burst into flames. Flames rode up his back and into his hair. He screamed and seized the blazing walking stick. With the stick held forward like a sword, he dove at Avers.

With speed almost beyond Booth's comprehension, Avers slid out the Colt from the back of his belt. He aimed and shot Booth once in the head before the red-hot tip of the walking stick touched him. Blood spurted out and sizzled in the flames behind Booth.

Booth crumpled back in front of Avers. His suit jacket was smoldering. Blood from the head wound put out any flames.

"The gun was empty," Cromie said aghast at the scene played before him.

"I reloaded while he babbled on. It was the only time I didn't mind him talking so much," Avers said as he flipped the body over and wrapped Booth's feet under his arms.

"Let's get out of here," Cromie said as he shoved his camera and plate inside the trunk.

"Don't lock it yet," Avers said dragging the burning body of the mad assassin behind him.

Dropping one of Booth's legs, Avers reached inside the trunk and pulled out the rope.

Cromie closed and locked the trunk. He yanked the trunk free of the burning house followed by Avers and his burden.

Several passers-by stared at the odd procession emerging out the burning mansion.

"I heard a gunshot," yelled a man hauling a cart filled with brightly colored clothes.

"We caught a thief, sir," Avers coughed, a bit of blood trickled out of the side of his mouth.

He lugged the body passed the few local residents seeking shelter from the fire. They just stood and stared at the two of them. One dragged a body. The other hauled a trunk. They resumed their trek to safety and gave the matter no more thought.

Cromie compared the loss of Arnold's library in the same scope of the fate of the Library of Alexandria.

Avers dragged Booth's body through the muddy street. He stopped in front of the brick mansion that was not burning.

He dropped Booth's legs. The body did not move. The mud smothered the flames.

As Avers tied the one end of the rope together, he said, "I knew he'd want a photograph of himself. His conceit demanded it. It was just a matter of time for him to set the stage for it."

"That's why you lugged this around the whole time?"

"As you'd put it, that's my racket. It was slowing us down otherwise," Avers replied as he slid the rope over the half-burned face with the hole in the forehead and around Booth's neck. He threw the other end of the rope over an extended arm of a nearby street lamp. Yanking the rope, he began to lift the body. Loss of blood weakened him to a degree that he couldn't raise the corpse off the ground.

Cromie placed his trunk behind the lamp post. For one more time, he stood alongside Avers. He gripped the rope. Placing his hands between Avers', he counted to three. Both of them jerked the rope hard and fast until they heard Booth's neck snap.

They tied the rope to the base of the lamp post. The partially burnt body swung from the radiating heat of the surrounding house fires.

Avers kept his vow to see Booth hang for his crimes. He was confident that justice was served. He had no doubt mankind was safe from Booth.

He glanced at his friend, smiled, and yielded to his wounds.

Cromie yelled for help in the flickering shadow of the nameless lynched thief.

EPILOGUE

Twenty hours later, it rained in Chicago. Nature accomplished what man could not—extinguishing the great fire that burned Chicago.

Four days later, an Army sentry opened a door to an office with simple furnishings. Philip Avers hobbled inside with a cane. His right thigh and shoulder were bandaged but he was well-rested and well-groomed.

He received an official invitation to First Congregational Church, temporary offices of Chicago City Hall. At Washington and Ann Streets, it was miles west of the devastated area. Transportation was provided for him as part of accepting the invitation. The main reason for accepting the invitation was to see his friend again.

"Good to see you again, Philip," greeted Cromie, standing up from a dark blue cloth arm chair. Cromie was sporting an expensive single-breasted suit. The two comrades gripped hands firmly and warmly. Smiles beamed forth at the sight of one another. They were genuinely grateful to be in each other's company once again.

"Richard, you look well. Did you recover anything?"

"No, but the Tribune bought all my photographs at a very, very generous fee. Quite a tidy sum, if I do say so myself."

The men sincerely enjoyed knowing each other had survived.

The last time they were in each other's company was in the early hours of the Great Chicago Fire. They were scorched and dirty. Avers passed out from the gunshot wounds and exhaustion. Cromie yelled for help. Immediately four men assisted Cromie and carried Avers to safety near Lake Michigan. The multitude also seeking shelter separated Cromie from Avers. Cromie and his trunk wound up spending the night near Lincoln Park in a vacated grave of an abandoned cemetery. Police transported Avers to Mercy Hospital on the south side.

Both were presented an invitation to come to temporary city hall offices. The note stated that both were invited. The chance to see each other again was something neither would refuse.

"I appreciate you both coming here at our request," boomed a voice behind a simple maple desk.

Instinctively Avers saluted General Sheridan who sat with elbows resting on the desk. Sheridan casually returned the salute. Standing behind him was an impeccably dressed long bearded man who Avers never met before. He judged him to be at least twenty years older than Sheridan

"At ease, Mr. Avers," Sheridan said grinning. "Please you and Mr. Cromie have a seat." Avers rested in the arm chair. Cromie remained standing.

"This is our good friend, the Honorable Mayor Robert Mason," Sheridan gestured to the man at his side.

"Mayor *Roswell* B. Mason," the man said, walking around the desk and shaking their hands with the practiced ease of a skilled politician.

"You may not be aware but I had to issue a proclamation putting Chicago under martial law with General Sheridan in command. That bastard, John Palmer, refuses to send in the National Guard to maintain general order and prevent lawlessness," Mason continued.

"The Illinois governor, it seems, is a political rival of our mayor," Sheridan explained.

Changing the subject, Sheridan added, "The purpose of this meeting is the city, the mayor and those of us in the United States Army want to acknowledge and thank you for the great service you performed."

"Our service?" Cromie asked suspiciously. Avers sat quietly.

"Mr. Avers, the intelligence you provided proved quite valuable. Please accept our apologies for not heeding your warnings sooner. The U.S. Army was able to limit the destruction in Urbana, as a direct result of your report. Only about fifteen blocks were damaged. The attack there began on October 9th, instead of the 8th, so we had time to heed your warning and sent down a small platoon. The others, however, were not prevented," Sheridan stopped, swallowing his words.

Roswell assumed the dialogue.

"Peshtigo in Wisconsin was the worst. I have, had, a lumberyard interest there so I've received details the next day. The entire town was destroyed. Total businesses wiped out. Families devastated. Estimates of more than a thousand may have died as a result. Some burned alive. Some drowned in the Peshtigo River trying to escape. In Michigan, the towns of Holland, Manistee, Port Huron – all burned to the ground."

Sheridan stood up to take control again.

"And thanks to you, we were able to track and confirm the Ku Klux Klan's involvement, their responsibility, their culpability. You provided the crucial impetus of this investigation. We would not have connected that organization to these criminal activities so quickly. President Grant will be taking further steps to dismantle that group. Federal agents will be sent to South Carolina next month to arrest Klan members."

Clearing his throat, Sheridan continued.

"The general public is unaware of the Klan's intention. We will launch an official inquiry into it next month. Except for Mr. Avers' report and Mr. Cromie's photographs, no other evidence exists of the Klan's involvement. You may have heard the various theories that people are espousing including that the fire may have been started by an anarchist group called the Societe Internationale or a spark from a chimney. Some crackpots actually claimed responsibility. One rumor is a cow kicked over a lantern."

The mayor stepped in. "A fire extinguisher salesman has even been blamed. The story goes that he wanted to demonstrate how useful his product could be."

"Well, the public should know the truth!" Cromie blurted out.

The mayor shook his head. "I'm sorry it's just not feasible at this time. Efforts have begun to rebuild this city. If it was revealed that the Klan's implication, more specifically John Wilkes Booth was not merely involved but started it. I mean, I mean, it would be detrimental to the cause, a black eye to the city."

"You know it was Booth. You know Booth was still alive?" Cromie gasped.

"Yes," said Mason. "Ahem, we've seen your photographs."

"He wasn't killed six years ago. You know that it wasn't a rabid delusion on my part," Avers said relieved, feeling vindicated.

Sheridan interrupted.

"We simply cannot have the American people lose faith in their government. They need not know Booth did not die in Virginia. That he lurked about undetected, skulking around unseen, planning attacks on American cities in retaliation. We just cannot have that!"

"The American people have a right to know!" Cromie insisted.

"I believe it would do nothing but do harm. At the very least distract from much needed recovery efforts," Mason said as he leaned close toward Cromie. "Besides, I know your publisher explained the situation to you."

"Mr. Medill paid me several thousands for my photographs," Cromie said.

"And they will never see the light of day," Mason finished.

The color drained from Cromie's face. "That's why the Tribune hasn't published any of them yet."

Mason shook his head. "They were never handed over to the Tribune. Didn't you find it odd that you dealt directly with the publishers and none of the editors?"

Sheridan leaned back into the chair behind the desk. "It was at his suggestion, not ours, of a large sum of money to help you get back on your feet. He was well aware that you lost everything in the fire. You were more than well compensated for a few photographs, weren't you?"

"So no other photographs exist. No one from the Times, the Post, the Republican. No one else from the Tribune. The fire burned for more than twenty-four hours. In all that time, no one with a camera took a photograph?"

Mason smiled. "Curiously enough, no other photographs exist. Medill completely understands how such a thing can negatively have an impact on the city's image and its reconstruction efforts. What was it he wrote in that editorial?"

Sheridan said proudly, "Chicago Shall Rise Again!."

Cromie turned to Avers. "Philip, help me out here."

"I do, in fact, agree with them, Richard."

"How can you! People died because of Booth. We saw two women die because of him!"

"I'm well aware of that, Richard. Don't you realize this will be Booth's greatest punishment? You witnessed the man's immense conceit first hand. Yes, he paid the price. Yes, justice was served. But a complete lack of acknowledgement of his role in this? You *know* how much he wanted credit for it. To be admired for it. He boasted of it. This is our way to deny that self-imagined glory. Let his death remain in the past. This is an opportunity to let his evil die with him. Make him inconsequential. That would be the final and most definite cutting blow to his vanity. The ignominy of it all and there is nothing he can do about it," Avers admonished.

Cromie's mouth opened and closed several times. He slumped deep in the luxurious chair.

Sheridan and Mason just stared at Avers like he was speaking gibberish.

Sheridan spoke up, "We are certain the Klan devised this plot, not Booth."

Cromie spoke up, "Remember, this wasn't the first conspiracy that Booth concocted. The plot to kidnap Lincoln in 1864 he formulated."

Avers nodded his head and said, "He may or may not have been one of the masterminds behind this catastrophe, but he definitely saw himself as the hero, the star of this elaborate stage production. I think how it would gall him if one of those Irish immigrants he so greatly despised was blamed for causing the fire and his part was lost to obscurity."

"Egad, you make him sound like that Greek myth, Narcissus. A child's story from school," Mason shuddered.

"You mean, that ridiculous fellow who fell in love with his reflection in the water?" Sheridan emphasized so not appear less educated than Mason.

"You, gentlemen, are well aware of his vanity as well as Richard and I. He assassinated the President of the United States in a theater filled with people. And rather than safely escaping the way he came, he dramatically leaps to the stage and delivered a line to an audience and exits offstage with an injured leg," Avers pointed out.

All three men stared at Avers without speaking another word.

After almost a full minute, Sheridan cleared his throat and shuffled the papers on the desk.

"Ahem, well, now to the purpose of this meeting. For meritorious service in alerting U.S. Army and federal government about the fires, Philip J. Avers is hereby re-instated at the rank of Lieutenant with back pay for a period of three years. A member of the staff at HQ has mentioned you may be amenable to this," Sheridan said.

Standing up and saluting, Avers said, "Yes, sir!"

"With Mr. Cromie and Mayor Mason as witnesses, you have agreed!"

Mason nodded. Cromie looked at Avers, realized that is what he wanted, and assented as well.

"Good. Your first order is do not talk, write, or in any way mention to anyone about John Wilkes Booth and his involvement in this travesty!"

Avers had no problem agreeing to that.

Mason turned to Cromie.

"Mr. Cromie, Richard, I would be greatly honored if you were to join my staff, in any capacity you desire," Mason said as he stuck out his hand.

"Your term is up before the end of the year, isn't it?"

"I'm certain my successor will find a place for you. I believe your Mr. Medill is interested in the office of mayor."

"At the same terms, to keep my mouth shut about Booth?" Cromie spat. He did not extend his hand.

Mason flabbergasted sputtered, "If it's a matter of money…"

"No, it is a matter of integrity, sir, as a journalist! That's my racket," Cromie said standing up and walking toward the door.

"As a journalist, your credibility will be called into question if you claim

John Wilkes Booth was alive. You have no proof. You can't verify it. No witnesses. No photographs," Mason smiled sympathetically.

"Richard, people have questioned not merely my credibility but my sanity because I said that Booth was still alive. For six years. I wouldn't wish that on anyone else, especially a friend," Avers sympathized.

Cromie froze and looked to Avers for support. Avers shook his head.

"You can't possibly believe that we should participate in this, this conspiracy, to defraud the American public about Booth," Cromie pleaded to his friend.

"You know where I stand on this, Richard. Disavow rather than denounce a vile murderer."

Sheridan leaned back in the chair and smiled.

"There's a post out west that can use a good man like you, Lieutenant. Even a possible promotion could be arranged."

Cromie looked at Avers with a disappointed sulk on his face.

"You mean, that's it? You're just going to let them get away with it?"

"Let who get away with what?"

"The government? The cover up!"

"What cover up?"

"That Booth was alive! The whole world needs to know."

"Why?"

"You chased this man for six years. Now you're selling out!"

"I didn't do for any other reason but to stop him. Booth is finally and definitely dead. Now that he's gone. That's been my focus, my goal, for six years. I've accomplished it," Avers leaned close to Cromie and spoke softly. "I'm taking that military post. Not as a payoff. But because I've got nothing else, Richard. I've accomplished my goal so it's time to move on." Avers turned to Sheridan. "I accept, General."

"Good to hear, son. After a few weeks of recuperation, we'll have the paperwork arranged. You'll be reporting to a colleague from West Point, very good friend of ours. Out west. Lt. Col. George Custer. He can always use a good tracker." Sheridan said clapping Avers on the shoulder.

"I don't know how good a tracker I am. It took me six years ..." Avers halted in mid-sentence.

Sheridan and Mason shook hands with Avers. He went to leave with Cromie. He turned the knob on the door but it was locked.

"Mr. Cromie, do you acquiesce to keep silent?" Sheridan asked.

Cromie did not look at Sheridan, Mason, or Avers, but nodded none the less.

Sheridan shouted, "Unlock the door, Sergeant."

The lock clicked and the armed guard opened the door. Cromie shot a glare back at Sheridan then to Avers. They left the makeshift office. Both wondering what would have happened if they did not agree to keep silent.

Outside the First Congregational Church, they encountered Mary Lincoln. At fifty-three years old, Mary maintained a youthful vigor. Just a couple inches taller than five feet, she was still considered attractive with her cherubic face and social standing.

Avers introduced Cromie to Mrs. Lincoln. They walked out of earshot of the soldiers waiting to transport them back to their temporary dwellings.

"It's an honor to meet you, madam. Your husband was a great man," Cromie said as he bowed to her.

She elegantly acknowledged him with a nod. "And thank you for your part in eliminating that inhuman filth. Philip informed me of how you helped to hang him for his crimes. And especially in your effort in saving our dear Philip."

"We also confirmed Tad was poisoned by that maniac as we suspected," Avers said.

"So that's it. The U.S. Army bought your silence!" accused Cromie.

"Richard!" said Mary indignant.

"I understand what he means, Mary," whispered Avers. "Like I said, Richard, for nearly six years this consumed me. Capturing Booth, making him pay for his crimes, was the only thing I had in my life. But no, they didn't buy my silence. I vowed to keep silent a long time ago. I didn't do it for the glory. I did it for the simple reason, it needed to be done. The federal government and the U.S. Army can rest knowing that Booth's death is now a fact. Mary's husband and son are avenged. The American public is safe and them knowing Booth was still alive makes no difference. The threat of Booth is removed permanently. And God willing so will any memory of him."

"How could you be so certain that he wanted the recognition for this disaster?"

"By the look on his face when I told him you were a reporter. I told you that's why I lugged that damn trunk around. It contained something he wanted. Booth lived for notoriety. That's why he repeatedly revealed himself. And the camera! Your camera allowed him a chance to reclaim his celebrity status. It was finally something I had that he wanted. His fate was inevitable. His arrogance was his downfall," Avers shrugged as if it blatantly obvious.

"But he'll bear no responsibility for the damage he's caused, the lives lost because of him!"

"Responsibility? You know he saw it as glory. Some others may see it as glory too. The way I see it the Ku Klux Klan will be dismantled with no martyr to hang their hat on."

"I can't stay in this town any longer, Philip. Medill gave me plenty of money to start over. I'll do so somewhere else. I'm heading east. Probably Michigan. Find out about what happened out there," said Cromie as he stuck out his hand to Avers.

The men grasped each other's hand and sighed. They shared a unique bond because of those eight hours. They knew they had to part ways and would never see each other again. The ordeal had changed them and its resolution separated them.

Cromie nodded respectfully to Mary Lincoln, turned on his heel, and left.

Mary turned to Avers and smiled.

"I hate to admit it, but he is right," she said. "Booth should be held accountable. I feel it is incumbent on me to force the government to accept its responsibility. Especially in regards to my son's death."

"Oh, Mary. Who would believe it? People would think you're crazy, much as they did me, for even uttering such."

"The government is not above the law. The truth is the truth, sweet Philip."

"Mary, dear Mary. History will say you're crazy then. You don't want your legacy to be that. I was shunned for six years, my sanity questioned, because of the truth. You were, perhaps, the first person to believe me in all those years."

"You know I will not be silenced, Philip," she grinned.

Philip Avers grinned back. "I know. No one tells you what to do, Mary."

"Thank you, Philip, for avenging my son," she said with a tear in her eye.

Alone on a planked sidewalk, they embraced. They embraced perhaps a little longer than social etiquette would approve. But no one would ever know. It was just another secret they would share.

"Now, get a decent suit to wear," Mary said as she pulled away and ambled toward her waiting carriage.

Ultimately, she would remain in Illinois and he would head west.

THE END

About Our Creators

Author

GEORGE TACKES—After graduating college with an English degree in 1983, George wrote plays in the 1980s that were performed at Chicago theaters. From 1990s, he was a newspaper reporter for suburban newspapers. In the early 2000s, he worked as an associate editor for trade publications. In 2018, George attended his first Windy City Pulp and Paper Convention and got the pulp bug. In 2021, Airship 27 published two of his stories in Sherlock Holmes Consulting Detective #17. He lives in Oak Lawn, Illinois with his wife, daughter and a very demanding dachshund named Bailey.

Interior Illustrator

GARY KATO—was born in Honolulu, in 1949. He graduated from the University of Hawaii with a Bachelor in Fine Arts degree. His comic book work has appeared in such varied titles as Destroyer Duck, Thunderbunny, Ms. Tree and Mr. Jigsaw. He's also illustrated children's books such as The Menehune of Naupaka Village and the currently available Barry Baskerville Returns and Jamie and the Fish-Eyed Goggles. He's also been a contributor to the Children's Television Workshop magazines, 3-2-1 Contact and Kid City.

Cover Artist

CHRIS RAWDING – is an eminent artist, educator and outdoor enthusiast. He has been a keen artist from his early days living on the South Shore of Massachusetts where he currently resides with his two sons. After attending the Museum School of Fine Arts and receiving his Bacherlor's in Commercial Illustration from the Art Institute of Boston, he now specializes in digital illustration, caricature design, branding and book illustration, as well as, screen printing and log design. His distinctive comic art style combined with his creativity and passion takes the subject matter to another level and uses color that don't exist in the real world, but makes them believable and turns them into edgy, eye-catching designs. As an eclectic visionary his gallery includes; pop culture, steampunk chic, superheroes and famous phantoms. For the past 20 years, he likes to take risks and pushes his concepts beyond the ordinary with a knack for modern, bold and organic design.

Murder Most Foul

In Volume 17 of Airship 27's most popular anthology—

A young boy's dog is cruelly slain. A British agent is murdered aboard a train and the daughter of a distinguished military officer commits suicide. These are just three of the five mysteries contained in this volume of new Sherlock Holmes adventures as offered by writers I.A. Watson, R.A. Jones, George Tackes and Jonathan Casey. Each offers the brilliant Holmes and his ever loyal companion, Dr. Watson, unique and exotic puzzles that will test their skills and bring them face to face with murder most foul.

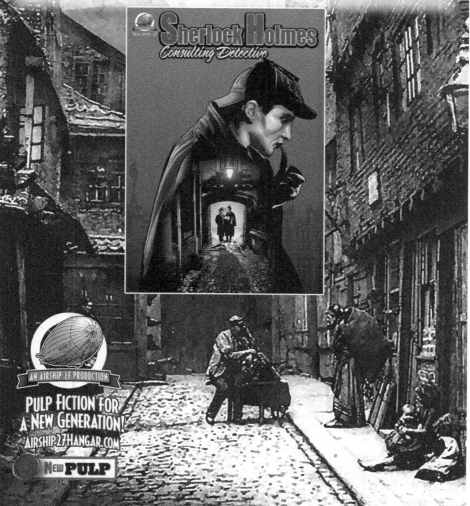

NIGHTMARE COUP

America's greatest fear is realized when President Trent's personal helicopter, Marine One, blows up with him aboard. At the same time, across the Atlantic, Air Force Two carrying Vice-President Duncan McNeil explodes while landing at Rome's international airport. Within hours a Palestinian radical fringe group called Vengeance claims credit for the assassinations. A shaken Speaker of the House, Oliver Holstein, is immediately sworn in as the new President.

Every intelligence agency of the free world is tasked with finding Husam al Din, the mysterious mastermind behind Vengeance. Then Italian officials report that the Vice-President's personal Secret Service agent miraculously survived the crash and is recuperating in a Roman hospital. What does he know? Can he provide intelligence that might uncover the inside agents responsible for the twin terror attacks? More importantly, is he still a target of Vengeance?

The stakes have never been higher as a cunning, ruthless foe prepares to unleash a nuclear holocaust on America's allies in the final Executive Gambit.

wayne carey
executive gambit

AN AIRSHIP 27 PRODUCTION

PULP FICTION FOR A NEW GENERATION!
AIRSHIP27HANGAR.COM

NEW PULP